Albert Barry

Life of Blessed Margaret Mary Alacoque of the Sacred Heart

Albert Barry

Life of Blessed Margaret Mary Alacoque of the Sacred Heart

ISBN/EAN: 9783744673303

Printed in Europe, USA, Canada, Australia, Japan

Cover: Foto ©Raphael Reischuk / pixelio.de

More available books at **www.hansebooks.com**

LIFE OF

BLESSED MARGARET MARY ALACOQUE

Nihil obstat.

JOANNES GIBSON, C.SS.R.,
Censor depulatus.

Imprimatur.

HENRICUS EDUARDUS,
CARD. ARCHIEP. WESTMONAST.

Die 9 Sept., 1889.

LIFE

OF

BLESSED MARGARET MARY ALACOQUE

OF THE SACRED HEART

BY

Rev. ALBERT BARRY, C.SS.R.

Permissu Superiorum

LONDON : BURNS & OATES, Ld.
NEW YORK : CATHOLIC PUBLICATION SOCIETY CO.
DUBLIN : GILL & CO.

THE ABERDEEN UNIVERSITY PRESS.

CONTENTS.

PREFACE.

HE beloved disciple Saint John said to Saint Gertrude, when he was asked why he had not made known to the world the wonderful sweetness which he had felt as he leaned his head in mystic sleep upon the Sacred Heart of Jesus Christ: "I was charged with the mission of instructing the infant Church concerning the mysteries of the Uncreated Word in order that these truths might be handed down to future ages, but it was reserved for a world grown cold in love to be aroused from its coldness and to be warmed anew by the knowledge of the throbbings of the Sacred Heart".

Devotion to the Sacred Heart always existed in the Church, and there were Saints who lived long before Blessed Margaret Mary of whom it was a noted characteristic. It was, however, reserved for the 17th century to spread it abroad among the faithful. That century had its Saints also, and the divine life of the Church showed itself then as of old. But heresy had made sad inroads into many lands, and the causes which produced it in them were at work elsewhere, and nowhere more than in France— that land whence went forth this, in a sense, new knowledge of the "sweet eloquence of the throbbings of the Sacred Heart".

The Church of France, it is true, was pre-served from the fate of that of England, but there is much to be deplored in the methods by which the disciples of gloomy Calvinism were silenced by Louis XIV. Far worse than the desecration of churches, the destruction of the sacred vessels, the slaughter of holy priests and religious, was the presence of the poison which the rude methods of an absolute monarch might, indeed, make harmless for the moment, but which was there all the same. Calvinism disappeared, but the pride and lawlessness from which it sprang passed into Jansenism, and wherever this subtle heresy appeared Christian virtues seemed to sicken and to die ; a monstrous growth took their place, and instead of a confiding love for God and a clinging to

and affection for Jesus Christ, there arose a
servile fear of God and a distrust of and a
disrelish for Jesus in the Blessed Sacrament.
Men of keen intellect, and of a power that has
hardly ever been surpassed of conveying to
others the ideas which had destroyed their own
faith, were at the head of this movement, and
soon a sad change passed over the land. The
forecast of the Apostle was then fully realised :
" In those latter days men shall become haughty,
proud, lovers of themselves, disobedient to
parents, slanderers and traitors ".

It was precisely at this time, when everywhere men's hearts seemed to have grown cold
and a torpor like unto death was stealing over
those who should have been sources of light and
love to others, that our Lord chose to put before
the world the treasures of His Sacred Heart.
And, as the decree of Beatification puts it, " In
order to establish and spread far and wide
amongst mankind this so saving a devotion, and
one so justly due from us, our Saviour vouch-
safed to choose His servant Venerable Margaret
Mary Alacoque, a Religious of the Order of the
Visitation of the Blessed Virgin Mary, who, by
her innocence of life and constant practice of

every virtue, proved herself worthy, with the aid of divine grace, of this exalted office and charge ".

How Blessed Margaret Mary was prepared for this work, how she overcame every obstacle from within and from without, is told briefly in the following pages, and yet at sufficient length to give the reader an opportunity of seeing how wonderfully beautiful her life was. There are many lovers of the Sacred Heart in this country, but not enough. If the faith is to spread abroad and fill the whole world, it must be more by the example of fervent Catholics than even by the preaching of the truth. There are numberless powerful agencies at work to spread the knowledge of the truth, but they everywhere lack the support which comes from fervent, prayerful, and mortified lives. Now, our Lord said of the result of this devotion upon all those who practise it :

I will bestow upon all of them the graces needful for their state of life.

I will establish peace in their families.

I will comfort them in their afflictions.

I will be their safe refuge during life, and especially at death.

I will bestow abundant blessings upon all their works.

Sinners shall find a fountain and a boundless ocean of mercy in My Heart.

Lukewarm souls shall become fervent.

Fervent souls shall quickly become very perfect.

I will bless every house where the picture of My Sacred Heart shall be exposed and honoured.

I will give to priests the power to touch the hardest hearts. Those who spread this devotion shall have their name written in My Heart, and it shall never be blotted out.

Saint Bernard writes: "O most sweet Jesus, what riches dost Thou contain in Thy Heart! How can it possibly be that men have but a slight feeling of the loss they suffer through their forgetfulness and indifference towards this loving Heart?" And Pius IX. also said: "The only hope of the Church and of society is in the Sacred Heart, for there we shall find a remedy for all our afflictions. Spread this devotion everywhere; it will save the world."

The Sacred Heart of Jesus Christ is a revelation of His love for us and of His sorrows for

our sake ; and the life of Blessed Margaret
Mary reveals to us our duty of making atonement to His Heart, which is wounded by the
wickedness of the ungodly and by the coldness
of those who profess to love Him. There is
nowadays a widespread conspiracy to destroy
the Christian world which was built upon the
Incarnation, and it behoves Catholics to make
reparation and expiation to the Redeemer for
the insults and wrongs which are daily done to
Him. All Catholics ought to be loving disciples
of the Sacred Heart, and to study to be like
unto It, and by their humility and their love of
Jesus Christ to shine brightly before the world.

As our Lord gave sight to the blind man by
means of clay, may He, through this little book,
bestow many graces upon those who read it and
who are led by it to love His Sacred Heart.

LIFE OF

BLESSED MARGARET MARY ALACOQUE.

CHAPTER I.

HER CHILDHOOD AND GREAT SUFFERINGS.

LESSED MARGARET MARY
ALACOQUE was born at Lhaute-
cour, in the parish of Verosvres,
of the diocese of Autun, July 22,
in the year 1647. Her father,
Claude Alacoque, was a royal
notary and judge in the baronial
courts of Terrau, Corcheval, and
Pressy. She was baptised three
days after her birth by her uncle, the parish priest of
Verosvres. She spent the first years of her childhood
with her father and mother, but she left home when
she was about four years of age and stayed for a few
years at Corcheval with her godmother, Madame de
Fautrieres, who dwelt in a large castle which was
situated at the foot of a hill about three miles from

Lhautecour, and was sheltered by a wood of elm trees, whose wide-spreading branches threw their shadow upon its time-worn walls. A small chapel stood in front of the mansion, and a lamp ever burned brightly in it before the Tabernacle where Jesus Christ dwelt in the Blessed Sacrament. Madame de Fautrieres entrusted the little child to the care of two of her waiting women, in order that they might instruct her in the catechism, and teach her to pray as well as to read and write. They fulfilled their duty faithfully, and taught her to love Jesus Christ and His holy Mother. They taught her that the Son of God had become man out of love for mankind, that He was born in a stable at Bethlehem, dwelt on earth for thirty-three years, and at length died for the salvation of men. They told her the wonderful truth that He still dwelt on earth, and that the God who once lay upon straw in the stable, whose words stilled the storm, whose look converted sinners, whose voice brought back the dead from the grave, whose body was scourged with whips, and His hands and His feet fastened with nails to the cross, still dwelt amongst men in the Blessed Sacrament; and that whilst hiding His lovely face He saw and heard, as when lying upon the straw in the stable He saw and heard the shepherds on that winter night at Bethlehem, and that there He fulfilled the promise: "Ask and you shall receive : if you ask anything in My name that I will do". They also taught her that Mary, the Mother of God and the queen of heaven, who is seated on a throne at the right hand of her Divine Son, clothed with the sun, with the moon beneath her feet, and a crown of twelve stars upon her head, was her loving Mother and protector.

The innocent child eagerly drank in their words, and thenceforth began to love Jesus and Mary with her whole heart. She delighted to linger in the silent chapel, and when wanted by anyone she was ever found kneeling with her small hands devoutly joined together praying before the Blessed Sacrament. She never grew weary of praying to Jesus and to His blessed Mother; and she always left with great sorrow the house of prayer where her beloved Jesus dwelt in the Tabernacle. She said the holy Rosary every day as well as she was able, and whilst saying it she knelt with bare knees upon the ground, and was wont to kiss the floor at each Hail Mary. She, however, said the Rosary one day seated, but the Blessed Virgin appeared and upbraided her with these words: "How is it, my daughter, that you serve me so slothfully?" Her heavenly Mother was well pleased with her child-like love and always watched over her, bestowed many graces upon her, and saved her from many dangers. She above all obtained for her, through her powerful intercession, a great fear and hatred of sin, and the little girl had such a fear of displeasing God by the slightest fault that it was enough for anyone to whisper to her the words, "That is displeasing to God," to check her at once when she was doing anything that was not altogether right. Many noticed that she kept aloof as much as she could from one of the women who had care of her, although she was kind and petted her, whereas she willingly stayed with the other woman, who had a somewhat bad temper and sometimes scolded her sharply, and it was discovered afterwards that the woman whom she thus disliked had not been leading a good life.

Margaret Mary spent four happy years with her godmother at Corcheval, but Madame de Fautrieres died in the year 1655, when she was only eight years of age, and she was sent back to the house of her parents at Lhautecour. Her home was a large rambling house with out-offices, and it was surrounded by a garden which was bounded on one side by a small wood which grew upon ground sloping down towards a narrow glen. The house where she dwelt was in the midst of green meadows which stretched away on all sides towards low rugged hills, which encircle that part of the rich plains of Burgundy, and these fields were broken here and there by huge granite boulders, by clumps of trees, and by ravines through which sparkling streamlets flowed, and were thickly studded with farm homesteads. The parish church of Verosvres, with its high roof and narrow windows, stood on rising ground at the distance of about half a mile, as if blessing the surrounding country, and the low-roofed dingy huts of the little village clustered around it as if seeking shelter beneath its ancient walls. Margaret Mary lived happily at home among her brothers and sisters, but God soon sent her the first of the many sorrows of her life. Her father died shortly after her return, leaving but little worldly wealth to his children, and his sorrow-stricken widow, having to give all her time to gather the money which many owed to him, was unable to watch over them. Margaret Mary was therefore sent to a convent of Urbanist nuns at Charolles.

Margaret Mary led such a holy life at the convent that she was allowed to make her first Communion when she was only nine years of age, and she had even already begun to think of becoming a nun. "It seemed to me that if I became a nun I should become holy like them, and I had so strong a wish to become a nun that I thought of nothing else. I, indeed, thought the convent where I was living not solitary enough, but as I knew of no other I thought that I should have to stay there. Our Lord mingled so much bitterness with all my little amusements after my first Communion that I found no pleasure in any of them, and whenever I was about to play with my companions I always felt drawn away and called into some quiet spot, and I had no peace of mind until I followed this impulse. I then felt myself forced to pray prostrate on my bare knees or making genuflections as long as I was not observed by anyone, for I very much disliked being seen doing these things."[1]

She, however, became very ill, and at length had to

[1] *Memoir.*

go back to Lhautecour, after having spent two years
at the convent. Her illness lasted for four years, but
she got many graces from God during these weary
days of suffering. " I felt strongly drawn to prayer,
but this attraction made me suffer much; for I
thought that I was not able to satisfy it, as I did not
know how to pray and there was no one to teach me.
I knew nothing of prayer except the name, and the
word *prayer* filled my soul with delight. The
Sovereign Master taught me how He wished me to
pray; He made me throw myself humbly before Him
and beg forgiveness for all my sins, and then, after
having worshipped Him, I prayed without knowing
how. He showed Himself to me in some mystery,
and I gave my mind so thoroughly to it that I felt no
distraction, and my heart was so filled with the desire
of loving Him that I yearned much for sufferings."[1]
Her illness baffled the skill of the doctors, but she at
length got back her health through the help of the
Blessed Virgin. " No other remedy could be found
for my ailment except to consecrate myself to the
Blessed Virgin: a promise was made to her that I
should one day become her daughter if I got back my
health. I had no sooner made the vow than I got well,
and thenceforth the Blessed Virgin watched over me in
a special manner."[1]

Her sufferings, however, were not yet ended.
Sufferings are the highway to heaven, and God has
said that He chastises those whom He loves, and His

[1] *Memoir.*

chastisement, as the Apostle writes, yields peaceable fruits of justice.

Her uncle, Toussaint Delaroche, took a lease of the property in the name of the children of Claude Alacoque, and he now had the whole management of the house and land. He with his wife and sister dwelt thenceforth at Lhautecour, and Margaret Mary and her mother were treated with great cruelty by them. "There was constant warfare, and everything was kept under lock and key, so that I was unable to get my dress to go to Mass. I had to borrow clothes. I felt this slavery very much. Things went so far that I could no longer do anything, nor even go out of the house without their leave. When I was in this state I felt drawn to seek comfort from the Blessed Sacrament of the altar; but as I was in a country house far away from the church I was not able to go there without their leave, and it happened that when one gave leave the other refused, and when I showed my sorrow by weeping they upbraided me with having made an appointment to meet some one, and with hiding it under pretence of going to Mass or to Benediction of the Blessed Sacrament. As I knew not where to find shelter, I used to hide in a nook of the garden or in the cow-house, or in some quiet spot where I might kneel, and, weeping, pour out my soul before God. I always did this through the mediation of my good Mother, the ever Blessed Virgin, for I had put all my hope in her. I used to spend the whole day there without food or drink, and the poor village folk out of pity sometimes towards evening gave me a little milk or fruit. I always went back to the house with such great fear and trembling that I was like a wretched criminal about to be sentenced. I would have preferred to beg my bread than to lead such a life, for I often did not dare to take it at table. The attack began more strongly than ever as soon as I had put my foot in the house, because I had not looked after the household work and the children of these dear friends of my soul, and I could not say a word in answer. I used to spend the night like the day weeping at the foot of the crucifix. My greatest sorrow was caused by being unable to lighten the load of sorrow of my mother, which was a hundred times heavier than mine. I did not dare to give her the comfort of speaking about it, for fear I should offend God by the pleasure of speaking of our sufferings. My grief was especially very great when she became ill, for she suffered much on account of being altogether thrown on my care and my services; and as everything was kept locked, I had to beg for eggs and for such things as are needful to the sick, and this was no slight torment on account of my natural timidity, especially with the village folk, who often received me very roughly. I had the sorrow of seeing that when my mother had got an alarming attack of erysipelas in the head they sent for a common village surgeon who happened to pass by in order to bleed her, and he told me that she could not recover from her illness unless by a miracle. I alone was distressed or

troubled by it. I was in constant affliction. I met
in the midst of it all only with mockery, ill-treatment,
and slander. I did not know to whom to go for help
or to whom I might speak save to my Sovereign
Master. I went to Mass on the Feast of the Circum-
cision of our Lord, to beg Him to be Himself the
physician of my poor mother and to teach me what I
should do. He so mercifully heard my prayer that
when I had returned home I found that the swelling
on the face had burst, leaving a wound as big as the
palm of the hand, and it gave forth a horrible stench.
Nobody would go near her; I had no experience in
dressing wounds; I could not before that time bear
even to look at or to touch them; I had no ointment
for dressing the wound on my mother's face; I merely
cut away every day a great quantity of bad flesh,
hoping all from the hands of Divine Providence. I
felt my courage and confidence in the goodness of my
Sovereign Master grow more strong, and He seemed
to be always by my side. The wound, contrary to all
human hope, was healed in a few days. I scarcely
ever went to bed or slept during the whole time
of the illness of my mother, and for many days I
ate hardly anything. My Divine Master comforted
and gave me strength by bestowing upon me perfect conformity to His holy will; for I had recourse
to Him alone during the whole time, saying to
Him: 'My Sovereign Master, this would not have
happened if it were not Thy will, but I thank
Thee for allowing it in order to make me like unto

Thee '." [1]   This downpour of sufferings caused
many lovely virtues to bud and bloom in her soul
and helped much to unite her to God. She thereby
gained great devotion to the Passion of Jesus
Christ, and He was ever before her mind either as
the Behold the man, or as bearing His cross to
Calvary, or as crucified upon it. Meditation upon
the sufferings and death of Jesus Christ strengthened
her to bear patiently her own afflictions, and she at
length gained so great love for sufferings and humiliations that when her rough relatives raised their
hands to strike her she was sorry when they forbore
to do so.

Margaret Mary felt more love day by day for the
Blessed Sacrament. "I could no longer say vocal
prayers in presence of the Blessed Sacrament, where I
felt myself so lost that I never grew weary of being
there. I would willingly have spent whole days and
nights there without eating or drinking. I did not
altogether know what I did, save that I melted away
like a lighted taper before Him, anxious to give Him
love for love. I was not content with staying at the
entrance of the church, but I failed not to go as near
as possible to the altar of the Blessed Sacrament,
although inwardly ashamed. I envied those who
could communicate frequently, and who could stay
before the Blessed Sacrament. I endeavoured to
gain the goodwill of those persons of whom I have
spoken, in order to get permission from them to go

[1] *Memoir.*

and spend some minutes before Jesus Christ in this mystery."[1] Margaret Mary had also a great thirst for prayer and contemplation, and would have spent her whole time in exercises of piety, but her relatives kept her working almost the whole day. Her will, however, was united to God during these weary hours of work. "I sought solitude as much as possible, in order that I might learn through silence how to love my Sovereign Good, who urged me to give Him a return of love for love; but I thought that I never could love Him as I should, no matter what I did, unless I learned to pray. I knew only what my Divine Master taught me, namely, to abandon myself to all His divine movements, whenever I was able to shut myself with Him in some quiet spot; but I was allowed hardly any time, for I had to work all day with the servants, and then in the evening it seemed as if I had not done anything to please those persons with whom I lived, and they so scolded me that I had no heart to eat, and I withdrew as soon as I could get a few minutes of peace which I so much desired."[1]

She was wont to betake herself, whenever she was able, to the little glen near the house, and there, kneeling at the foot of a huge granite rock, and hidden from sight by the grove of trees, she prayed, with her eyes turned towards the parish church, the apse of which she could see in the distance. This pure-minded maiden of fifteen years, forgetful of earth, with its sins and sorrows, spent hours in this

[1] *Memoir.*

lonely glen, praying to Jesus Christ, who dwelt in the
Blessed Sacrament in silence and in solitude. She
also became very fond of penance, and not only fed
her soul with prayer, but severely chastised her flesh,
and brought it into subjection by fasting, by scourging
herself, and by sleeping on the bare ground. She
always watched and prayed the whole of Christmas
night, out of love for the Holy Child. Christmas Day
was for her a renewal of the day when the Divine Babe
lay on straw in the stable of Bethlehem, worshipped
by Mary and Joseph and the shepherds, and she
welcomed Him by receiving Him in Holy Communion.
She was in the parish church one Christmas morning,
yearning wistfully for His coming, but the parish priest
forbade all who had not slept during the night to
communicate, so that the day of joy became for her a
day of tears.

Margaret Mary had made a vow of virginity when
she was a child; for one day, when hearing Mass
kneeling, as she always did, on her bare knees, even
when the weather was bitterly cold, she, at the time
of the consecration, said, " My God, I consecrate my
purity to Thee ; I vow perpetual chastity to Thee ".
But her mother now besought her to marry. " My
mother was ever endeavouring to get me to marry. I
beheld her weeping when she used to say to me that
she had no hope of escape from the misery in which
she lived, except through me ; that she would be
happy if she could go with me when I should be
settled in the world. God, however, left my heart no

peace. I had my vow always before my eyes, with
the thought that I should be punished by awful
chastisements were I to go against it. The devil
took advantage of the tender love which I had for
my mother, putting before me unceasingly the tears
she wept, and that if I became a Religious I would
make her die of grief, and that I would have to answer
for it to God, as she was given over entirely to my
care and services. This made me suffer frightfully,
for we loved each other so tenderly that we could not
bear to be out of each other's sight. The wish to be
a nun, on the other hand, was ever pursuing me,
together with a horror of the least impurity. All this
made me suffer a real martyrdom. I had no rest,
and was ever weeping, and I knew not what to do,
as there was no one to consult. At length the tender
love which I had for my mother began to gain the
upper hand. My God, Thou alone knowest the
length of this terrible warfare which went on within
me. I would have yielded, were it not for the extraordinary help of Thy mercy." [1] She, however, held
steadfast to her promise, and did not yield to her
mother's entreaties.

God made her go through this purgatory in order
to purify her soul, for " gold and silver are tried in the
fire, but acceptable men in the furnace of humiliation ". These trials, afflictions, and trouble of mind
refined her soul, and made it like unto Jesus Christ.
" O souls, who seek your own ease and comfort, if you

[1] *Memoir.*

knew how needful sufferings are for this high state, and how useful afflictions and mortifications are in order to obtain these great blessings, you would never seek comfort anywhere, but would take up the cross with the vinegar and gall, and would consider it a priceless blessing, knowing that by thus dying to the world and to your own selves you are about to live with God in spiritual gladness.   God deals thus with those whom He means to exalt.   He allows them to be tempted, afflicted, tormented, and chastened, both inwardly and outwardly, to the utmost limit of their power, in order to make them, so to say, divine, and to unite them to Himself in His wisdom ; as it is written : 'The words of the Lord are pure words ; silver, tried by the fire ; purified from clay ; seven times refined '."[1]

[1] St. John of the Cross.

CHAPTER II.

ARGARET MARY, having been tried by adversity, was now tried by prosperity. Her brother came of age in the year 1663, when she was sixteen years old, and he became master of the house. Her uncle, Toussaint Delaroche, had made the property valuable by his skilful management during ten years, and the family was once more wealthy. Her mother, who was again in her rightful place at the head of the household, wished her children to marry, and therefore invited much company to the house. Margaret Mary began then to love the world and its pleasures, and the good seed in her heart was smothered by them. "I began to see company and to dress in order to please them, and I sought amusements as much as I could. I committed great sins, for once I disguised myself at Carnival time from a foolish desire to give pleasure."[1] Saint Francis of Sales writes: "Amusements, balls, feasts, dress, outward adornment, are not in themselves evil, but these

[1] *Memoir.*

things are dangerous, and to be fond of such things is opposed to devotion and very dangerous. It is not a sin to do these things, but it is a sin to give oneself immoderately to them. It is a pity to sow in the garden of our heart such vain and foolish affections which take the place of virtuous impressions, and hinder the sap of our souls from feeding our good desires. We can never be fond of them without injury to devotion. The heart of man overloaded with these useless and dangerous affections cannot go forward swiftly towards God."

Margaret Mary unhappily had set her heart upon worldly amusements, and her eagerness for them dimmed the brightness of her devotion, and over-clouded her soul. She drank freely at first of the wine of earthly pleasure, but in the end it filled her with bitterness and poisoned her exercises of piety. God also upbraided her in the depths of her heart for her unfaithfulness to Him, and she heard His voice saying to her, as He had formerly said to the Jews : " My people have done two evils : they have forsaken Me, the fount of living water, and have dug cisterns for themselves ; broken cisterns that can hold no water ". Her conscience thus reproached her in the midst of the gaieties of the world ; and when at night she had laid aside her worldly dress, she beheld with her soul her Divine Lord covered with blood as if after His scourging, and heard His divine voice saying to her that her vanities and worldliness had brought Him to that state. The thought of the severe account that she should have to give at death, and of her ingratitude in betraying Him who had shown such great love to her, inflicted so deep a wound upon her heart that she used to weep bitterly, and, throwing herself upon the floor of her room, she with great sorrow begged His forgiveness, and then most severely scourged herself in order to make some satisfaction for her sins. The warfare between the flesh and the spirit, nevertheless, still went on, for, although the spirit was willing, the flesh was weak, and for two years more she continued to yield to her fondness for worldly amusements. She sought in vain to serve two masters, foolishly hoping that God would accept a half-hearted love. "I used to bind this wretched body with knotted cords in order to take vengeance on my flesh on account of my sins, and I used to tie them so tightly that I could hardly breathe or eat. I left them on me for so long a time that they became embedded in my flesh, and I could not take them off without a great effort and cruel torture. I did the same thing with small chains with which I bound my arms. I could not remove them without tearing away bits of flesh. I slept at night upon a plank or upon rough logs of wood."[1] After torturing her body in this manner at night, she gave her heart to pleasure again the next day, but God did not want mortification of the flesh so much as love of the heart. The constant struggle going on within her heart between love of God and love of the world made her

[1] *Memoir.*

lose her health and waste away. She, however, was at length startled from her spiritual slumber by the angel of death.

Margaret Mary lost at this time her two elder brothers, both of whom she tenderly loved. John, the eldest, died in the flower of his youth in the year 1663, and Claude, the next eldest, died at the age of twenty-three years in the year 1665. When the shadow of death fell upon her she was awakened from her day-dreams of worldly happiness, and she ceased "to love vanity and to seek after falsehood,"[1] and began to have her conversation in heaven. The desire of becoming a nun once more grew up in her heart, and it at length became so strong that she resolved at every risk to leave the world and enter a convent. She began then to read the Lives of the Saints, but always sought for those whom she could more easily imitate, and she often wept when she thought how they either had not been guilty of sin or else had done penance for their sins.

She gave alms and endeavoured to do all the good she was able to do to the poor children of the neigh-bourhood. "I used to give all my money to poor children in order to coax them to come to the house that I might there teach the catechism as well as their prayers to them, and so many came that I did not know in the winter time where to assemble them."[2] She used to teach them in a large room at the top of the house near her own room, as it could be entered

[1] Psalm iv. [2] Memoir.

from the outside by a stone staircase.　Her brother,
Chrysostom, one day seeing a throng of children at the
house, said to her : "My dear sister, do you then
intend to become a schoolmistress?"　She answered,
"If I do not teach them who will do it?"　Her aunt
sometimes rushed out of the house and angrily drove
them away.　"They thought that I gave to the poor
whatever I could lay hands on, but I would not have
dared to do so through fear of theft.　I had to caress
my mother in order that she might allow me to bestow
my own.　She readily gave me leave, for she was very
fond of me."[1]　Margaret Mary knew that "religion
clean and undefiled before God and the Father is this :
to visit the fatherless and widows in their tribulation,
and to keep oneself unspotted from this world".[2]
She, therefore, visited the poor and afflicted in their
homes.　"I loathed the sight of sores.　I forced myself to dress them, and even to kiss them, in order to
overcome myself.　I was not skilled in dressing them,
but my Divine Master knew so well how to make up
for my want of skill that these sores were soon healed
even when they were very malignant.　I, therefore, had
more trust in His goodness than in the remedies
which I used."[3]

She yearned for some calm harbour where her soul
might be sheltered from the storms of the world ; and
she wished to give the fragrant flower of her virginity
to God, whilst it was still sweet with the morning
dew and unstained by the dust of earth, in order that

---

[1] *Memoir.*　　　[2] St. James ii. 27.　　　[3] *Memoir.*

she might be found worthy one day to be with the 144,000 virgins who follow the Lamb whithersoever He goeth. She wished to deny herself, to take up the cross, and to follow Jesus Christ to the mountain of myrrh, in order that with a soul white as snow and a body shining with purity she might some day be betrothed to Him and become His bride by a supernatural union. But her elder brother, Chrysostom, who was now head of the family, and had wedded a daughter of one of the chief families of the neighbourhood, was anxious that she should marry and settle in the world. Her mother also besought her with tears to wed one of the many youths of good family, who eagerly sought her hand, and to take her with her to her new home, for she was unwilling to dwell under the same roof with her daughter-in-law. "I was unable to withstand any longer the persecutions of my relatives and the tears of my mother, who loved me so fondly, and who urged that a girl of twenty ought to settle in life. The devil also kept ever saying to me, 'Poor wretch, what do you mean by wishing to be a nun? You will become the laughing-stock of the world, for you never can persevere, and how ashamed you shall be when you put off the religious dress and leave the convent. Where will you go and hide?' I began to yield to the views of my mother that I should settle in the world, but I could never think of it without weeping, for I felt an unsurmountable dislike of marriage."[1] She, however, feared that if she

[1] *Memoir.*

became a nun she would no longer be able to pray, to give alms, to fast, and to take the discipline as she liked, and that, moreover, she would never reach the high holiness of the religious life, and that, therefore, she should undoubtedly lose her soul. She began to examine her vow of virginity, and she thought that she was not bound by it, as she had made it when she was a child, without understanding fully what she was doing, and that, at least, she could easily be freed from it. She was thus held fast by the slender thread of natural affection, and was unable to fly to Him, to whom she had plighted her troth. "How sad it is to behold some souls like ships richly freighted, full of good works, of spiritual exercises and virtues, and gifts of God, which never reach the harbour of perfect union, because they have not the hearts to break off certain tastes, attachments, or affections, and yet it would need but a single vigorous effort to break the thread of their attachment." [1]

God, however, spoke strongly to her heart. "He showed me one day after Holy Communion that He was the most lovely, the wealthiest, the most powerful, the most perfect, the most accomplished amongst all lovers, and that having promised myself to Him how could I seek to withdraw from Him. Be well aware that I will forsake you for ever if you thus scorn Me, but I will not forsake you, and will give you victory over all your foes if you are faithful to Me. I excuse your ignorance, for you do not as yet know Me, but I

[1] St. John of the Cross.

will teach you to know Me and will manifest Myself
to you if you are faithful." These thoughts or words,
spoken deep down in the depth of her soul, filled her
with peace, and she felt as if the chains that bound
her had been broken. As soon as the storm in her
soul had been thus stilled by the words of Jesus
Christ, she renewed her vow of virginity, promising
that she would never be aught else than a Religious
even were it to be at the risk of her life, and she said
aloud, "Who will give me the wings of a dove that I
may fly and be at rest?" Jesus Christ, having in this
way sweetly and gently moved her heart by His holy
inspirations, poured out His graces in great abundance
upon her, and He so attracted her and drew her to
Himself by the strong power of His merciful hand,
and by the sweet enticements of His grace, that she
yielded up her freedom to Him and made Him
master of her whole self. She told her mother and
her relatives of her resolution as soon as she had gone
out of the church, and she besought them not to
hinder her design and to send away all the suitors for
her hand. "My mother, seeing this, did not weep any
more when I was present, but whenever she spoke
about it to other persons she was always weeping, and
they failed not to come to me, and to say to me that
I would cause her death by leaving her, and that I
should have to answer to God for it, and that I might
as easily become a Religious after her death as during
her life. A brother also who was very fond of me
did his best to make me give up my design, and he

offered me a part of his inheritance to help me to settle in the world, but my heart had become as immovable as a rock." [1]

Margaret Mary, however, was forced to spend three years more in the midst of the wicked world, and her mother sent her to live in the house of her uncle at Mâcon, where she might have the distractions of a city life. She made the acquaintance, whilst she was there, of his daughter, who was a nun in the Ursuline Convent in the town. Her cousin and the other nuns often besought her to become a nun in their convent, but she said to them : " If I entered your convent it would be merely out of love for you ; but I wish to go somewhere where I have neither relatives nor friends, so that I may become a Religious through love of God ". Her uncle wished her to stay with him, for he loved her as if she were his child ; and he would not allow her brother to take her home, saying that he had a right to keep her, as he was her guardian. Her brother, who was unwilling that she should become a nun, was very angry, for he thought that it was a trick in order that she might enter the convent in spite of him. But she had no intention of becoming an Ursu-line nun ; and the more strongly the nuns entreated her the greater was her dislike, for she heard in her soul a voice saying, " I do not wish you there, but at Holy Mary ". She, however, was not allowed to go to the Visitation Convent, although she had relatives in it ; and many stories hurtful to the good name of

[1] *Memoir.*

the convent were told to her, but the more they sought to hinder her the more she wished to enter it. She says : " I was attracted by the lovely name of Holy Mary, and I felt that I should find there what I sought. When looking one day at a picture of the great Francis of Sales, he threw a loving and fatherly glance at me, and at the same time whispered in my heart the word ' Daughter'. I, however, dared not to speak of it ; and I knew not how to free myself from my cousin and from the whole community ; and they showed me so much friendship that I would not have been able to keep from entering among them had not God given wonderful help to me. They were going to open the gate of the monastery when I heard that my brother was very ill, and that my mother was dying. I had to set out at once to go to them ; and they could not hinder me, although I was myself un-well. But this was rather sorrow at seeing myself forced to enter a convent where, as I thought, God did not call me than anything else. I travelled the whole night, although it was almost ten leagues ; and thus I got free." [1] She watched over her mother and her brother with loving care, and they both slowly regained their health. Margaret Mary meanwhile was strongly urged not to become a nun, and some priests said to her that her mother could not live without her, and that she would have to answer to God for her death. She suffered much through her affection for her mother, and the devil also tempted her by

[1] *Memoir.*

the thought that it would bring her to everlasting
ruin.

Margaret Mary was helped by the Blessed Virgin in
all her troubles. "The Blessed Virgin was ever a
mother to me, and never failed to help me. I had
recourse to her in all my difficulties and needs ; and
I went to her with so much confidence because I
thought that I had nothing to fear under her maternal
protection. I made a vow to her to fast every Saturday, and to say the Office of her Immaculate Concep-
tion as soon as I should be able to read it ; and to
genuflect seven times every day of my life, together
with seven Hail Maries in honour of her seven
sorrows ; and I consecrated myself to her to be
her slave for ever, begging her not to refuse to
receive me as such. I spoke to her as a child
with simplicity, as if to a good mother, for whom I
then felt myself full of a truly tender love." [1] She got
great help also from the Sacrament of Confirmation,
which she received in the year 1669, when she was
twenty years of age. She remained unshaken in her
desire to be a nun, and she delighted to think of the
spiritual advantages of the Religious life. "My
chief delight was to think that I could receive Communion frequently, for they seldom allowed me to do
so. I would have thought myself the happiest person
in the world if I could communicate frequently and
spend the night before the Blessed Sacrament. I felt
myself on the eve of Communion buried in such deep

[1] *Memoir.*

silence that I could not speak without an effort from the greatness of the action which I was about to perform ; and after it I cared neither to eat, or drink, or look, or speak, so great was the consolation and peace which I felt." [1]

Margaret Mary did not waste her time in vain repining at not being able to become a nun, but endeavoured to lead the life of a nun at home in order to fit herself for the convent life which she hoped to have some day the happiness of leading. She practised silence, obedience, and mortification. She meditated much on the sufferings of Jesus Christ, and was eager to imitate them. " I used to bind my fingers tightly, and then pierced them with needles so as to give Him some drops of my blood. I took the discipline every day in honour of His scourging ; I would willingly have cut myself in pieces on the last three days of Carnival in order to atone for the insults which sinners gave to his Divine Majesty ; I fasted as well as I could on bread and water on these days, bestowing on the poor whatever was given to me for my food." [1] She knew that spiritual direction was needful, and she prayed fervently to God to send her some holy priest who would guide her soul aright. God heard her prayer, and a Franciscan father of great holiness, who had come in the year 1671 to preach the jubilee in the parish of Verosvres, stayed for some days at Lhautecour in order to enable the members of the family to make general confessions.

[1] *Memoir.*

Margaret Mary was so full of sorrow for her sins that she wept very much and would willingly have made them known to the whole world. She spent fifteen days writing her general confession. " I wrote every-thing that I could find in books about confession; and I sometimes wrote things of which I had a horror of even pronouncing, but I said to myself, I have perhaps done it without knowing it. I made my confession to this good father, but he would not let me read the whole paper, but made me skip several pages, although I earnestly besought him to allow me to satisfy my conscience, being a greater sinner than he thought."[1] She told something about her manner of life, but not all, from fear of giving way to vanity ; but she made known her desire to become a nun, and how she had been hindered by her family for several years from fulfilling the will of God. He gave her good advice, taught her to pray, promised to send some instruments of penance to her, and encouraged her to follow faith-fully the Religious vocation which had been given to her by God. He then spoke strongly to her eldest brother, Chrysostom, and bade him forbear from going against the will of God. Chrysostom was frightened by his words, and, seeking for his sister, asked her whether she was still bent on becoming a nun. She answered, " Yes ; I would rather die than change ". He soon afterwards went to Mâcon to make arrangements for her entrance into the Ursuline Convent in that town. " My brother went to arrange

[1] *Memoir.*

about my dowry with my cousin, who never ceased
urging me. My mother also and my other relatives
wished that I should be a nun in that convent. I no
longer knew how to save myself; I had recourse to
my good mistress the Blessed Virgin, through the
intercession of Saint Hyacinth, to whom I prayed a
great deal. I also had many Masses said in honour
of my Holy Mother. She one day said to me lovingly,
' Fear nothing, you shall be my true daughter, and I
will always be your good mother '. These words gave
me delight, and freed me from all doubt that my desires
should be fulfilled in spite of all opposition." [1] Her
brother, as soon as he had returned, said to her :
" They require to have four thousand livres for your
dowry. It is for you to do what you like with your
money, as the agreement has not yet been ratified."
She answered boldly : " It shall never be ratified ; I
wish to go to the Holy Maries in some convent
far from here, where I have neither relatives nor
friends, for I wish to be a Religious only from love
for God. I wish to forsake the world altogether,
and to be forgotten by it, and never to behold it
again." [1]

Margaret Mary went shortly afterwards to bid
farewell to her former teachers in the Urbanist
Convent at Charolles. They took her into the
house, and, gathering around her, endeavoured to
persuade her to stay amongst them, saying that she
was their beloved daughter, and that they could not

[1] *Memoir.*

bear to see her enter the Holy Maries, as they knew that she could not persevere there ; and they made her promise to come back to them when she should have left it. She however remained unmoved, and was determined to live and die under the shadow of the convent tower of Holy Mary. When she returned home her mother and elder brother allowed her to choose whichever Visitation convent she liked best ; and they read a list of convents of that order in France. As soon as she heard the word Paray-le-Monial her heart swelled with gladness, and she at once chose that house as the place of her abode. She went there shortly afterwards with her brother in order to pay a visit to the nuns there. " I went as quickly as possible to the place of my happiness— to beloved Paray." [1]

Margaret Mary had no sooner entered the convent parlour than she heard, deep down in her soul, the words : " It is here I wish you to be " ; and she then said to her brother : " You must certainly come to an agreement, for I will never go elsewhere ". He was surprised, for he had no intention of allowing her to stay there ; but she was unwilling to depart until everything had been settled, and he had to yield to her earnest entreaty. As soon as a settlement was made, and she was accepted by the nuns as a postulant, her heart overflowed with happiness ; and her inward joy showed itself so much outwardly that those who knew not what was passing in her inmost

[1] *Memoir.*

soul, seeing her so cheerful and merry, said : " Look
at her ! How very unlike a nun she is !" She returned with her brother to Lhautecour in order to
make the needful preparations for forsaking the world
for ever. She stayed at home for a month, and on
the evening of her departure, June 19, she made her
will, in which she bequeathed all her worldly goods,
with the exception of her dowry, to her mother, to
her younger brother, and to the three daughters
of her elder brother, together with a small sum of
money for buying a banner or chasuble for the parish
church.

Margaret Mary left her home for ever the following
morning, and set out with a joyful heart for Paray-le-
Monial, which was about twenty miles distant from
Lhautecour. "The long-wished-for day at length
came when I was to bid farewell to the world. My
heart never felt such gladness and strength ; it was in
a manner insensible to friendship as well as to the
sorrow shown by my relatives, and especially by my
mother ; and I did not shed a tear when I left them.
I felt as if I were a slave set free from chains and
prison in order to enter the house of her Spouse : to
possess it and to enjoy His presence, His goods, and
His love, with full freedom." [1] She thought when she
looked for the last time at her home, at the parish
church, where she had so often prayed, and at the
green fields, where she had so often wandered in her
youth, that the Religious life, like the kingdom of

[1] *Memoir.*

heaven, was a pearl of great price, and that it was wise
to sell all that she had in order to buy it. She heeded
neither the weary road over which she slowly went,
nor the scorching sunbeams of the midsummer sun,
but, overflowing with happiness, she thought only of
that fountain of living water where she hoped to slake
the thirst of her soul ; and she wistfully sighed for the
moment when, having fled from the storms of the
world, she might, like a dove, build her nest on high,
in the hollow of the rock, sheltered from wickedness
and from sin. When, after travelling the whole day,
she had reached a little before nightfall the brow of
the hill around whose wooded slopes the road gently
wound, she beheld beneath the small town of Paray-
le-Monial stretched out amid green meadows, watered
by the river Bourbince, and girded by graceful plane
trees, with its narrow streets and houses, and the steep
roofs and lofty dormer windows of the Visitation Convent, and the three grey towers of the ancient abbey
church glowing under the mellow rays of the setting
sun. But as she was entering the peaceful harbour,
after having been tossed so long on the wild waves of
the world, a dark cloud overshadowed her like the
sunset gloom then settling on the golden valley at her
feet, and her soul overflowed with sadness. " When
the time had come for entering the monastery, which
was on Saturday, I was assailed by so great agitation
that my soul seemed as if it were leaving my body.
However, I had no sooner gone in than my trouble
ceased, and I saw that our Lord had stripped off the

sackcloth of my captivity and had clothed me with the garment of gladness. I was truly so much out of myself for joy that I exclaimed : ' It is here that my God wishes me to be ! ' " [1]

[1] *Memoir.*

CHAPTER III.

HE Visitation Order was founded by Saint Francis of Sales and Saint Jane de Chantal, in the year 1610. Saint Francis wrote: " I hope that this Congregation will be a sweet and happy refuge for those who have not strong health, for without much bodily austerity there is the practice of every essential virtue. They say the Office of Our Lady, and make their meditation, work, keep silence, practise obedience and humility, have nothing of their own, and lead a life as loving, peaceful, interior, and edifying as can be seen in any convent in the world. After this profession they will go with great humility, God willing, to visit and serve the sick." He called them the Congregation of the Visitation, because they were to be uncloistered and to seek their work; but such was not the will of God, and they afterwards became cloistered and contemplative. Saint Francis wished the nuns to take the Sacred Heart of Jesus Christ as their model, and to be always simple, humble, and gentle. " I have always thought that to fulfil the

purpose for which our Congregation of the Visitation was established, and to understand better the special spirit of the Visitation, that it was a spirit of deep humility towards God, and of great gentleness towards our neighbour. Their hands are busy gathering, at the foot of the Cross, the little virtues of humility, gentleness, and simplicity, which grow there and are bedewed with the blood of their Beloved." He gave them the " Sacred Heart " as their coat of arms. He wrote on the Friday after the Octave day of Corpus Christi, June 10, 1611, these words to Saint Jane de Chantal : "Our house of the Visitation has now sufficient nobility by His grace to have its own escutcheon, arms, and motto. I have thought, therefore, my dear Mother, should you agree with me, that we should take for our coat of arms a heart pierced by two arrows and encircled by a crown of thorns, this poor heart serving as a base for a cross surmounting it, and having the holy Names Jesus and Mary engraven upon it." He also wrote : "The nuns of the Visitation, who shall be so happy as to keep their Rule well, may truly bear the name of evangelical daughters established in these latter days to imitate the Heart of Jesus in meekness and humility, the base and foundation of their Order, which will give them the privilege and the surpassing grace of being daughters of the Sacred Heart of Jesus". The Order of the Visitation spread rapidly, and soon there were Visitation monasteries in France, Italy, Bavaria, and Flanders ; and a monastery of the

Visitation was founded at Paray-le-Monial, in the year 1626, during the lifetime of Saint Jane de Chantal, chiefly through the exertions of the Jesuit Father Paul de Barry. A splendid convent was built for the nuns in the year 1642, in the midst of a beautiful meadow beneath the shadow of the ancient Abbey Church of Saint Hugh of Cluny, which had stood on the green hillside for six hundred years watching lovingly over the little country town. This convent formed four sides of a square, and a cloister decorated with inscriptions, according to the advice of Saint Francis, went all around, having a small court with a fountain in the midst ; and the choir, refectory, novice room, and community room opened upon it, whilst two staircases at the angles led to the first storey where the narrow, whitewashed cells of the Religious were situated. A large garden, with straight, well-shaded walks, stretched from the convent walls towards the east.

Margaret Mary entered this convent as a postulant, June 20, 1671, at the age of twenty-three years, and, two months later, became a novice. The convent contained at that time thirty-four choir nuns, three novices, and six lay sisters. Rev. Mother Hersant, who had known Saint Jane de Chantal, and had been for twenty years under the guidance of Saint Vincent de Paul at Paris, was the superior, and Rev. Mother Thouvant, who had been a nun at Paray for forty-four years, and had been blessed by Saint Jane de Chantal when she was a novice, was novice

mistress. Saint Jane de Chantal had foretold of her
that she would do very great good in the Order by
her prudence and by her religious virtues. Margaret
Mary, as soon as she had entered the convent gate,
which she was never to pass through again as long as
she lived, felt keenly the great sacrifice of worldly
pleasures which she was making, and understood
fully the life of hardship which she was beginning to
lead ; but she had made up her mind to become a saint
at any cost. " I felt at once engraved on my soul
that this house of God was a holy place, that all who
dwelt there should be saints, and that the very name
of Holy Mary showed that I must be one at any cost ;
that I should, therefore, give myself to God without
hesitation, and sacrifice myself to Him without reserve.
This thought made all that at first seemed hard become sweet to me."[1] She was filled with the desire of
giving herself altogether to the service of God, and
she went the next morning to the novice mistress and
asked her what she should do in order to pray, for
she declared that she did not know how to pray, and
the novice mistress, who could not believe that
having entered Religion at the age of twenty-three she
should be ignorant of it, merely said to her, "Go,
place yourself before God as a blank canvas before a
painter".

When the great plague of 1628 had reached Paray-le-
Monial, one of the nuns, having been struck down by it,
was carried out to a little hut built in a corner of the

[1] *Memoir.*

garden, and another sister chosen by lot was shut up with her in order to nurse her. The sick sister one day, whilst suffering very much, cried out aloud, " O gentle hand of my Spouse, paint, paint," and when the superior asked her what she meant, she answered, " My mother, I am placing myself before God as a blank canvas before a painter : I beg Him to paint in me the perfect likeness of my crucified Jesus ". Margaret Mary did not clearly understand the meaning of these words, but she went away in order to kneel before our Lord and pray. " I would have liked her to explain her command more fully, for I did not understand it, and I did not dare to tell her so. But I heard inwardly these words : ' Come and I will teach you '. And, indeed, I had no sooner knelt down to pray than my Sovereign Master let me see that my soul was the canvas where He would paint all the features of His life which had been spent in love, silence, and sacrifice, unto the end ; but that to make this picture He should first cleanse it from all the stains adhering to it, and from love of earthly things as well as from self-love and love of creatures, towards which I had a great leaning." [1]

Margaret Mary thenceforth sought to crucify her flesh in every way that she could. She even went too far, for having got leave one day from the novice mistress to do some act of penance, thirsting to wash out all stains from her soul by tears and by penitential works, she resolved to do more than she had

[1] *Memoir.*

4

permission to do; but Saint Francis of Sales in a wonderful way reproved her for her want of obedience.
Saint Francis one day, when speaking to his nuns,
had said to them that if they should forget the spirit
of moderation and sweetness in which he wished
them to live in order to give themselves to bodily
penances in opposition to the Rule, he would come
back to life and make such a noise in their cells that
they would understand that they had acted contrary
to his wishes. He now kept his word towards Margaret Mary, and, although he had been dead for many
years, he spoke to her strong words of rebuke. "My
blessed Father chided me so sharply for overstepping
the bounds of obedience in this matter, that I have
never had courage to do so again. 'What, my
daughter,' said he. 'do you think that you please
God by going beyond the bounds of obedience?
It is obedience and not the practice of mortification
which upholds this Congregation.' These words
have remained ever engraved on my heart." [1]

Margaret Mary was clothed with the religious habit
August 25, in the year 1671. She wrote that day in
the convent register these words: "I, Margaret Mary
Alacoque, the daughter of the late Claude Alacoque
and of Philibert Lamyn, my father and mother, being
twenty-three years of age, with my free will, and with
the leave of my mother, after having dwelt for two
months within the house, having seen and considered
its Rules and exercises of devotion, have freely asked

[1] *Memoir.*

to be received to the habit among the choir sisters of this Congregation, and I have obtained it by the grace of God, having with the habit changed my name and received that of Margaret Mary, to-day, August 25, 1671. Sister Margaret Mary Alacoque." She was very modest and humble, and a holy joy beamed on her face whilst she was going through the ceremony of reception as a novice. She looked on herself as thenceforth espoused to her Divine Master, and our Lord filled her soul with such sensible devotion that she was almost beside herself, and could hardly do any work. She showed always a wonderful joy and fervour during her noviceship, and the novice mistress, beholding her so happy, tried her with many mortifi-cations and humiliations, but she always received them without saying a word and with a joyful and cheerful countenance. She even begged for humiliations, although she felt them keenly. "Although I did not get those for which I asked, I got others which I did not expect, and which were so contrary to my own inclination that I was forced, on account of the effort I had to make, to say to my good Master, 'O Lord, come to my help, for Thou art the cause of this'."[1] Our Lord failed not to hear her prayer and helped her to bear these trials with patience, and He made known to her that He would always help her if she kept her own nothingness and weakness ever buried in His strength.

Margaret Mary had always had an extraordinary

[1] *Memoir.*

aversion for cheese, and her brother, when making
arrangements for her entrance into the convent, had
made an agreement with the nuns that they should
not require her to eat it. The novice mistress, however, one day reproached her for not eating it like the
other members of the community, but she could not
bring herself to do so. "It seemed to me, on the one
hand, that the sacrifice of my life would have been a
thousand times easier than this; and only that I
loved my vocation more than my life, I would have
given it up, rather than make up my mind to do what
was required of me. I felt, on the other hand, that
my Sovereign Lord wished for this sacrifice from me,
because so many others depended on it."[1] She
struggled hard during three days to overcome herself,
and all who saw her were filled with pity. She at
length went to her novice mistress in order to eat it,
but she lost courage, and full of sorrow she said,
"Alas! would that I might rather die than fail in
obedience". The novice mistress told her that she
was not worthy to do it, and that now she would not
be allowed to do it even if she wished. Margaret
Mary, hearing this, said within herself, " I must either
conquer or die," and she went at once to the church,
and kneeling before the Blessed Sacrament, said,
"'Alas, my God, hast Thou forsaken me? Must there
be any reserve then in my sacrifice, and shall not
everything be burnt as a perfect holocaust?' My
Divine Master, wishing to try to the utmost the

[1] *Memoir.*

fidelity of my love to Him, took pleasure, as He afterwards made me know, in beholding divine love fighting against the repugnance of nature in His unworthy slave. But love at last was victorious, for without any other consolation or arms than these words, 'There must be no reserve in love,' I went and threw myself on my knees before my mistress, begging her in pity to allow me to do what she had wished me to do. I did it at last, although I have never felt so great a repugnance to anything, and this came back every time I had to do it. This went on for about eight years."[1] God, in reward for this great sacrifice, then gave her an overflow of graces and of consolations. " I do not mention here all the abundance of divine grace with which I was visited, because it was so great that I could not tell it in words." [1]

She had one more struggle with her natural affections, for she had an affection for one of her fellow-novices, and she thereby put a hindrance to union with God ; because "if this earthly affection increases that of God cools down, and men forget Him by reason of that affection of sense, and remorse of conscience results ".[2] Jesus Christ made her know that He did not desire a divided heart, and that He would withdraw from her unless she withdrew from creatures. She then, by a great effort, broke off this particular friendship, and gave herself entirely to His love.

[1] *Memoir.*   [2] St. John of the Cross.

Jesus Christ began thenceforth to treat Margaret Mary as His beloved child, and He enriched her with many wonderful gifts and supernatural graces. He drew her to Himself and filled her with His love, and she beheld Him with the eyes, not of her body, but of her soul, always present at her side. "I beheld Him, I felt Him near me, I heard Him better than I could do with my bodily senses. He honoured me with His discourse, sometimes as a Friend, or as a Spouse full of love, or as a Father wounded with love for His only child, and in other characters."[1] She spent hours praying, and her pale face often had at that time a supernatural brightness. She was so wrapt up in the thought and the love of God that she could do hardly any work : things fell from her hands, and she seemed beside herself, to the wonder of the nuns and of her fellow-novices. "It happens sometimes that our Lord imperceptibly infuses a certain agreeable sweetness into the depths of our soul, which witnesses to His presence, and then the faculties, and even the outward senses, of the soul, by a certain hidden pleasure, turn in towards that inmost part where the most amiable and beloved Spouse is dwelling; for as a young swarm of bees, when it takes flight and changes its place, is recalled by a sound made softly on metal basins, by the smell of honied wine, or by the scent of some sweet-smelling herbs, being stayed by the attraction of these agreeable things, and going into the hive got ready for it ;

[1] *Memoir.*

so our Saviour, pronouncing some hidden word of His love, or pouring out the odour of the wine of His predilection, more delicious than honey, or allowing the perfumes of His garments, that is, the feelings of His heavenly consolations, to enter into our hearts, and making them thereby perceive His most welcome presence, draws unto Him all the faculties of our soul, which gather around Him and keep themselves in Him as in their most desirable object. And as he who would cast a magnet amongst many needles would at once see them turning all their points towards their well-beloved loadstone, and cling to it ; so when our Saviour makes His most delightful presence felt in the midst of our heart, all our faculties turn their points towards it, in order to be united to this incomparable sweetness. But when the union of the soul with God is most specially strict and close, it is called inhesion or adhesion by theologians, because the soul is caught up by it, is fastened, glued, and affixed to the Divine Majesty, so that she cannot easily free herself or draw herself away again. Look, I beg you, at that man, whose attention is caught and attracted by the delight of harmonious music, or perhaps, however extravagant, by the folly of a game of cards : you would wish to withdraw him from it, but you cannot ; he cannot be forced away from it, no matter what business awaits him at home, and even food and drink are forgotten. O God Theotimus, how much more ought the soul which is in love with its God to be held fast and tightly bound, being united to the divinity of the infinite sweetness, and seized and wholly possessed by this object of incomparable perfections."[1]

Margaret Mary was closely bound and united in this manner to her beloved Lord and Master Jesus Christ, and was ever absorbed in the thought of Him. The novice mistress, however, was bewildered, and at length warned her that her life was not in keeping with the spirit of the Visitation Order, and she threatened that she should be sent away unless she gave up her extraordinary ways and did everything like the other novices. Margaret Mary did her best to obey, but she failed notwithstanding all her efforts. " I did my best to follow the method of prayer which they taught to me, together with the other practices ; but nothing stayed in my mind. I vainly read the points of prayer, for all vanished, and I could not learn or remember anything except what my Divine Master taught me. And this made me suffer much, because they undid, as well as they could, all His workings in me, and I strove as much as I could against them."[2]

Margaret Mary was made assistant to the infirmarian sister, and this sister, who was more like Martha than Mary, and was naturally very fond of work, was ordered not to spare her. She was not allowed to stay in the choir, and as soon as the meditation had been read she had to go and sweep the corridors, arrange the cells, and weed the garden ; and when

---

[1] St. Francis of Sales.   [2] *Memoir.*

she asked leave to pray she was roughly sent away. "After this work, when I went to ask my mistress for leave to resume my prayer, she roughly sent me away, saying that I had made my prayer by doing the work of the noviceship. I did this work without being distracted from the sweet joy and consolation which my soul enjoyed, and which I felt increase daily. I was ordered, after hearing the points of the morning meditation, to go away and sweep the part of the court marked out for me until Prime. I had to give an account after Prime of my prayer, or rather of that which my Sovereign Master made within me. I felt inwardly an extreme pleasure in all this, as I had no other intention but to obey, however great the pain I thereby suffered in my body. The gladness with which I overflowed was so great that I could not keep from singing."[1] As she went about with a broom or a duster in her hand, whilst the nuns were praying quietly in the convent choir, she contemplated Jesus Christ, and listened to His silent whisperings in her soul; and grace bloomed in her like a beautiful rose-bud beneath the warm rays of the summer sun.

Rev. Mother Hersant ceased to be superior of the convent on the Feast of the Ascension, 1672, and she declared before leaving for Paris, whither she had been recalled, that Sister Margaret Mary would reach a very high degree of holiness, but that she did not seem to be altogether suited for the Order of the Visi-

[1] *Memoir.*

tation. Her successor, Mother Mary Frances de Saumaise, who was then fifty-two years of age, and of whom Saint Jane de Chantal had foretold that she would be among the best superiors of the Order, at once noticed the humble and fervent novice and saw in her signs of the Spirit of God. She nevertheless would not allow her to make her vows when the year of her noviceship had ended, for the nuns disliked her extraordinary ways, and the wise superior feared that she was unfit to be a Visitation nun. Saint Francis of Sales one day, after having celebrated Mass, had knelt with Saint Jane de Chantal at the foot of the altar, and they had prayed together to God that He would never send any extraordinary grace to the Congregation ; and the Saint had often entreated the nuns to keep strictly to the Rule, without ever going beyond it. It thus became a settled conviction amongst the nuns of the Visitation that they ought to live a hidden and peaceful life, and be like humble little violets growing beneath the shade. The superior and the novice mistress saw that she was most humble and obedient, mortified and burning with love of God, living, as it were, already in heaven, going about with a modest look, with her eyes always cast down to the ground, ever willing to work, and rejoicing in suffering and humiliations. They nevertheless feared to allow her to consecrate herself to God in the Visitation Order, and the 25th of August came and went, and Margaret Mary was still a novice. She complained gently to Jesus Christ. " I represented to my Sovereign

Lord these reproaches which I received, and complained to Him, saying, 'O Lord, wilt Thou then be the cause of my being sent away?' I got the following answer from Him : ' Tell your mother superior that she need not fear to receive you, and that it is I who give this assurance to her '." [1]

The mother superior, as soon as she was told this, bade her pray to the Lord to make her useful to the Order by an exact observance of all the Rules. She prayed, and the Lord granted her petition. "His loving goodness said to me : 'My daughter, I grant to you what you ask. I will make you more useful to the Order than they think, but in a manner as yet known only to Me, and I will suit My graces henceforth to the spirit of your Rule, and to the will of your superiors, and to your own weakness, so that you may receive with suspicion whatever withdraws you from the strict observance of your Rule, which I would wish you to prefer to everything else. I am willing, moreover, to prefer the will of your superiors to My own, when they forbid you to do what I have bidden you to do. Let them do as they like with you, I shall know how to make my designs succeed, even by the very means which seem opposed to them. I keep to Myself the guidance of your interior, and especially of your heart, in which I have established the kingdom of My pure love, and I will never yield it to anyone." [1] Margaret Mary gave herself thenceforth wholly to strict obedience and exactness in regular observance. And

[1] *Memoir.*

it was decided at length that she was fit to make the holy vows of Religion and to become a professed nun of the Visitation Order.

Margaret Mary began the retreat before her profession towards the end of the month of October, in the year 1672, and she spent the ten days preceding it in wonderful silence, recollection, and union with God. She became, after two days, so lost in contemplation that it was thought necessary to distract her, and she was entrusted with the charge of watching an ass and its foal that were kept in a corner of the garden, and of carefully hindering them breaking into the kitchen garden. She was thus ever on the move, endeavouring to keep them from trampling on and eating the plants, and she did this work most cheerfully, although she would have been glad to spend her time in the choir, praying before the Blessed Sacrament; because she hoped to find God and to get His graces whilst thus busy doing His holy will; and she said: "If Saul found the kingdom of Israel whilst searching for his father's asses, why should not I get the kingdom of heaven whilst running about after these animals?" She indeed got a wonderful favour from God at this time; for one day, when she was kneeling down amidst some hazel trees in the garden, our Lord gave her a clear knowledge of His sacred Passion. "I was so happy with this work, and my Lord kept me such faithful company, that I had never experienced anything like it. He especially made me understand about His holy Death and Passion; but it is an abyss to write about, and its length makes me omit it. I shall only say that it has given me so great a love for the Cross that I cannot live for a moment without suffering—but to suffer in silence without consolation, alleviation, or compassion, and to die with the Sovereign of my soul overwhelmed beneath the Cross of all kinds of insults, neglect, humiliations, and contempt."[1]

Whilst she was praying before the Blessed Sacrament, on 2nd November, she offered herself to Jesus Christ, and begged Him to receive her as a holocaust, and to unite this sacrifice to the sacrifice which He had made of Himself to His Eternal Father; and He made known to her that when she espoused a crucified God she must bid farewell to all the pleasures of the world: be blind, deaf and dumb to all earthly things, and consider her body as not existing; that she should fasten herself to the cross which He would send to her, and that it would be so heavy that without the help of His arm she could not bear it. He, however, at the same time, bestowed upon her the sweet manna of heavenly consolations and gave gladness to her heart. She was filled with that wonderful peace which is given by God to those who love Him. "I enjoyed such peace at night, even when very tired and weary, that my only uneasiness was lest I should not love God enough. I spent the whole night with such thoughts. No time was so pleasant for me as the night, for it was the most fitted

[1] *Memoir.*

for speaking to my Beloved. I therefore begged my guardian angel to awaken me from time to time. I then felt my heart wholly filled with God, whose speech was so sweet to me that I often spent three hours without any other movement or feeling save love, and I could not fall asleep again."[1]

[1] *Memoir.*

CHAPTER IV.

AINT FRANCIS OF SALES had taught that a novice should have a good heart, a good mind, and a good will to go forward in perfection, and profit by the remedies given during the noviceship, in order to be fit to become a nun. Margaret Mary had fulfilled these conditions; she had gone swiftly onwards upon the road of perfection, and her soul was now in the full beauty of spiritual bloom. She loved God alone with her guileless mind and spotless soul, and she was the most lovely flower in that garden of the Lord. The long desired day when she should consecrate herself wholly to her beloved Lord at length dawned, and, kneeling behind the iron bars of the grille in the convent choir, she made the three solemn vows of Religion, November 6, in the year 1672. She was now a professed nun of the Visitation Order: a stainless virgin in that very illustrious portion of the flock of Christ: a member of that chaste and chosen race then serving God with great holiness in the Convent of Holy Mary at Paray-le-Monial. She was now the bride of Jesus Christ, and He said to her : "Hitherto I have been thy Betrothed : henceforth I will be thy Spouse". She wrote with her blood on the day of her profession the following words: "I, a poor wretched nothing, declare unto my God that I will offer and sacrifice myself to everything which He demands of me ; offering my heart entirely to fulfil His good pleasure without making any account of any other interest save His greater glory and His pure love. I consecrate and give my whole self and every moment of my life to this. I belong to my Beloved for ever as His slave, His handmaid, and His creature. He is wholly mine, and I am His unworthy spouse.

"Sister Margaret Mary henceforth dead to the world.

"Wholly from God, and nothing from myself.
Wholly to God, and nothing to myself.
Wholly for God, and nothing for myself."

Margaret Mary felt, during the whole of that happy day of her espousals with Jesus Christ through her Religious profession, as if she were standing upon Mount Thabor ; but before nightfall the bright scene was overshadowed by Calvary, for she received a weighty cross which, according to nature, she keenly felt. She, however, does not mention in her *Memoir* in what it consisted.

Margaret Mary was ever closely united to God by prayer, and she overflowed with His sweetest consolations; but above all she was very humble and mortified. Saint Francis de Sales had written: "To be a Religious is to be fastened and doubly fastened to God by a continual mortification of self, and to live for God alone: our heart, tongue, and hands being always busy in the service of His Divine Majesty. Religion is nothing else than a school of self-denial and mortification." Margaret Mary understood this teaching, and loved contempt, humiliation, and suffering. She strewed ashes on her food, placed rough boards and broken earthenware in her bed, and "she would have destroyed her body by watchings, disciplines, and other sorts of penances had she been allowed".[1] She often kissed the sores and the ulcers of the sick, and she once wiped away with her tongue the vomit of a nun who was afflicted with cancer in the stomach. She said whilst doing this: "My Lord, if I had a thousand bodies, a thousand loves, a thousand lives, I would willingly sacrifice them all in Thy service". She felt drawn and strengthened by the sweetness of divine inspirations to perform these heroic acts of virtue, for, "even as a tender mother leading her little babe assists and supports him as need requires, letting him now and then venture a step by himself in less dangerous and very smooth places, now taking him by the hand and steadying him, now taking him up in her arms and bearing him; so our Lord has a continual care to conduct His children, that is, such

---

[1] Mother de Saumaise.

as are in charity, making them walk before Him, reaching His hand to them in difficulties, and bearing them Himself in such labours as He sees would be otherwise unsupportable to them. He declared this by Isaias, saying, "I am the Lord thy God who takes thee by the hand and says to thee, 'I have helped thee'".[1] The love for Jesus Christ which was enkindled in her soul made all these mortifications and sufferings sweet to Margaret Mary, and she gladly ran swiftly onwards upon the path of perfection.

The nuns of the Visitation Order led a contemplative life; they were like Mary who sat motionless and silent, listening with her whole mind to the words of Jesus Christ, whilst her sister Martha worked eagerly for Him. They, like Mary, had chosen "the better part," and their lives flowed on like a gentle stream amid the meadows, free from the care of temporal things, and undisturbed by worldly thoughts; happy in the contemplation of the perfections of God : yet they worked as well as prayed. They spent whatever spare time remained after contemplation, which is called by Saint Bernard "the work of works," in household drudgery, watching the sick, teaching the children who dwelt in the convent, and in various works by which they earned money for the support of the community. Some of the nuns painted, others embroidered, others plied the distaff, and others worked at the loom or made shoes and clothing for

[1] Saint Francis of Sales.

their sisters in Religion.   Margaret Mary also worked
like the rest; but while she worked she prayed, and
her mind was ever bent upon God and heavenly
things.   She worked for the glory of God, and her
work became a prayer; for, according to the ancient
monastic saying, "to labour is to pray".   She however was very fond of praying, and when she had to
cease praying in order to work, she felt as if her heart
was being torn from her body.   She was strongly
tempted to impatience one Easter Sunday morning,
because she was hindered by her occupations from
being present at prayer with the rest of the community, but Jesus Christ inwardly rebuked her, and
told her that He was more pleased by the prayer of
obedience and sacrifice than by contemplation.   She
was accustomed when going to her work to say: "My
Jesus, as I cannot stay any longer in Thy presence,
come with me to sanctify all that I do, for it is all done
for Thee".   He heard her prayer, and even when most
busy at work her mind and heart were always united
to Him.   "This divine presence filled me so fully
with a feeling of abasement, that I felt myself
drowned, as it were, in the abyss of my nothingness,
from which I have never since then been able to free
myself.   As I was filled with reverence for His
Infinite Majesty, my own inclination would have led
me to remain always prostrate on my face or on my
knees before Him; and indeed I always kept that
position as far as my work and my weakness allowed.
His Divine Majesty never let me stay in any less

respectful posture, so that when I was alone I never dared to remain seated."[1] It was indeed noticed by the nuns that Margaret Mary always knelt, and was always as recollected, as if she were in the church when she was working, reading, or writing, and the convent school children were wont to come stealthily and to peep at her as she knelt at her work, entirely lost in contemplation of God.

Margaret Mary spent all her spare time before the Blessed Sacrament. The Blessed Sacrament is the most wonderful work of God upon earth, being not only a perfect picture and representation of Jesus Christ, but Jesus Christ Himself still dwelling amongst men. He once lay on straw in the stable warmed by the breath of the ass and the ox, and Mary and Joseph saw Him gently sleeping, with closed eyelids and motionless limbs, in the manger. He now is a prisoner in the Tabernacle bound fast by His love for men. A few heaven-enlightened men then knelt at His feet in the stable by the wayside, and now some sinless souls come like the Shepherds and the Wise Men and pray to Him in His prison, where He waits day and night to give them comfort, and consolation, and encouragement to go forward bravely on the narrow road to the eternal kingdom. Margaret Mary knew that Jesus Christ was as truly in the Tabernacle as He had once been in the stable at Bethlehem, and she came as often as she was able and knelt for hours

[1] *Memoir.*

with clasped hands and uplifted eyes before the
Blessed Sacrament. She sometimes spent the whole
day praying in the choir before the altar where her
beloved Jesus dwelt. She knelt motionless, unconscious of all around her, like a marble statue,
her face lit up with a heavenly light and her cheeks
often bedewed with tears. She prayed thus every
Sunday and festival day from early morning until
dinner-time, and, again, from the end of the afternoon recreation until Vespers. She prayed before
the Blessed Sacrament every Holy Thursday from
seven o'clock in the evening until four o'clock,
and sometimes even later, the following morning,
and she never grew weary, and, like the blessed
in heaven, never ceased to make acts of love and
adoration to Jesus Christ in the mystery of His
love.

The Religious used to come during the night and
gaze at her through the half-opened door of the choir
as she knelt in prayer profoundly recollected in God,
and the school children who dwelt in the convent often
begged earnestly to be allowed to leave their beds and
watch their holy mistress at her prayers. A nun one
day said to her, " How can you remain so long kneeling in the same posture?" And she answered, smiling :
" I am so intent upon the Passion and Death of the
Lord that I do not know whether I have a body or
not, for I do not feel it ". She, indeed, had so crucified her flesh and its concupiscences, and had become
so pure and perfect and so detached from love of self

and of creatures, that she was able to behold the spiritual world almost as if her soul, already freed from the prison-house of the body, were beyond the grave and enjoyed the sight of God in heaven. Her bright faith brought her to the feet of Jesus Christ in the Blessed Sacrament, and kept her kneeling there for hours, and gazing upon Him with the eyes of her spotless soul, like Mary Magdalen at the foot of the Cross, or the beloved disciple Saint John when he leaned his head upon the breast of his Divine Master, and listened to the throbbings of His Sacred Heart. As the lofty mountain-peaks glow in the gleam of the morning sun, so her soul, having reached very high perfection, was wonderfully enlightened, and the Divine Presence shone brightly upon it, and she then learned to know and to love the Sacred Heart of her Sovereign Lord and Master. He became to her like a lovely vale where she never grew weary as she wandered amid its green and purple bowers and shady paths, watered with gently flowing streams and musical with the sweet melody of birds singing their summer songs, and she would willingly have spent her lifetime kneel-ing at His sacred feet whilst she contemplated His beauty and listened attentively to His sacred words. She, however, knew that perfection chiefly consists in obedience to the will of God, and she sought rather to please her Beloved Lord than to surfeit herself with spiritual sweetness. She, therefore, at once left the feet of Jesus Christ at the least sign from her Superiors. A sister once whispered in her ear, as she was thus praying fervently in the choir: "My sister, our mother wishes you to go and warm yourself at the fire". She immediately arose, genuflected reverently to the Blessed Sacrament, and went to where the fire was blazing, and, having stayed there during a quarter of an hour, she went back to the choir and remained there in prayer until the following morning.

CHAPTER V.

FIRST VISION OF THE SACRED HEART.

(A.D. 1673.)

ARGARET MARY thus walked worthy of God, pleasing Him in everything, being fruitful in good works, and ever growing in His knowledge and love. Her soul was a lovely garden full of the fairest flowers. The bitter wind of suffering had blown through it, but the warm south wind of spiritual sweetness had also blown through its flower-beds, and the flowers of virtue bloomed and gave forth a delicious fragrance, and Jesus Christ, her beloved Spouse, beholding the garden of her soul full of heavenly riches, came down from heaven and took delight in it. "My Beloved has gone down into His garden to the bed of aromatic spices, to feed in the garden and to gather lilies."[1] Her Spouse, thenceforth, often spoke familiarly and lovingly to her soul. She felt herself surrounded by the presence of God and became lost in an ecstasy of love whilst she was praying in presence of the Blessed Sacrament on the Feast of Saint John,

[1] Canticle of Canticles, vi.

December 27, in the year 1673; and she beheld with
the eyes of her soul the Sacred Heart of Jesus Christ,
shining like the sun and transparent as glass, having
upon it the wound which it had received on the cross:
it was encircled by a crown of thorns and there was a
cross above it. Jesus then said to her: "My Divine
Heart is so full of love for men, and especially for you,
that, unable any longer to keep within Itself the flames
of Its burning love, It needs must spread them abroad
through means of you, and It must make Itself known
unto them in order to enrich them with the treasures
which It contains. I make known to you the worth
of these treasures: they contain the graces of sanctification and of salvation which are needful to free them
from the abyss of perdition. I have chosen you, who
are an abyss of unworthiness and ignorance, to carry
out this great work, so that it may be seen that everything has been done by Me." He then said to her:
"Hitherto you have borne only the name of My slave,
I now bestow upon you that of beloved disciple of My
Sacred Heart". Margaret Mary remained all on fire,
as it were, after having received this wonderful favour,
and for many days she could not speak. She felt a
vehement pain in her side which caused such agony
that it hindered her sleeping at night, and this pain
became greater on the first Friday of every month.
For a long time after having received this vision of the
Sacred Heart, and having heard these words, she was
altogether lost in an ecstasy of love. "I knew not
whether I was in heaven or on earth. I was so beside

myself that I could not, without a great effort, come to
myself again in order to speak, and it needed a great
struggle to take part in recreation or to eat."[1] She
was so filled with the thought of God that she could
hardly explain herself to the mother superior, and she
had a vehement longing to throw herself at the feet of
her sisters and make known all her sins to them. "It
would have given me great comfort to make a general
confession aloud in the refectory, in order to let them
see the great heap of rottenness that was in me, in
order that they might not give me credit for the graces
which I had received."[1] This vision, instead of exalt-
ing, humbled her, and filled her with a lowly opinion
of herself; she not only got a more lively feeling of
her sinfulness and worthlessness, but forgot all the
good she had ever done during her lifetime, and her
only thought and wish was to give honour and glory
to Jesus Christ. She knew that the vision which she
had received had been given to her through the goodness of her beloved Lord, and she sang, like the
Blessed Virgin Mary: "My soul doth magnify the
Lord, and my spirit hath rejoiced in God my Saviour,
for He hath regarded the lowliness of His handmaid".
᛫ Visions may come, indeed, from the imagination or
from the devil as well as from God. As Saint Teresa
writes: "There are persons, and I know many, whose
imagination is strong and their mind works so vividly
that they think that they behold distinctly everything
that comes into their mind, whereas, if they had had

[1] *Memoir.*

true visions, they would know, without a shadow of doubt, that their visions were but fancies, and, as they are merely the word of the imagination, they not only have no good effect, but leave them colder than would the sight of a pious picture ".[1] "The imagination and fancy of some persons," writes Saint John of the Cross, "are full of imaginary visions, whether it be the result of the great strength of that faculty which, after the slightest effort of the mind, represents and pictures the usual forms in the imagination : whether it be the work of the devil, or whether it be the work of God. We, however, may know their nature by their effects. Those that are natural or diabolical in their source do not produce good effects, nor do they spiritually renew the soul, whereas those that come from God produce some good effects whenever they are remembered. The effects of these visions in the soul are peace, light, joy akin to glory, sweetness, purity, love, humility, and inclination or elevation of the mind to God."[2] The ideal or spiritual vision of the Sacred Heart, represented by light infused from on high, which was granted to Margaret Mary, and the words whispered by Jesus Christ in the depths of her soul, produced wonderful effects in her, and strengthened her greatly to advance in virtue, to become more spiritual, more united to God, and detached from herself. As a painted fire gives neither light nor warmth to the body, so this vision if it were the work of the imagination would not have given light to her mind and warmth to her heart, but, being the

[1] *Interior Castle.* [2] *Ascent of Mount Carmel*, iii. 12, ii. 24.

work of God, either directly or by the ministry of an angel, it gave her new strength and new life to do His holy will. When the brilliant sun shines at spring-time, trees and shrubs grow green, flowers bud and bloom, and the birds pour out a merry song, so Margaret Mary grew in holiness and gave forth most lovely and fragrant flowers of humility, mortification, and love for God and for her neighbour.

Margaret Mary was ever cheerful, peaceful, and happy, and was altogether free from every desire of being known or esteemed. She by the strength of her will held a firm sway over her feelings, and she constantly performed very severe penances. She subdued her flesh and its unruly appetites, and so became more spiritual every day, and more fit to receive the supernatural favours of God. Jesus Christ, by His grace, perfected first her bodily senses, moving her to make a good use of outward things, such as hearing Mass, and sermons, and mortification in food and drink, together with chas-tisement of the flesh. She perfected her senses by severe penance, for yielding willing obedience to the inspirations of Jesus Christ she chastened her body with hair-shirts, girdles studded with iron spikes, fasting, and scourging unto blood; and she chose spoiled fruits, crumbs of bread that had fallen on the floor, and badly cooked meat, for her food, pouring cold water upon it in order to make it tasteless. God then perfected her soul by His holy grace, bestowing supernatural favours and con-

solations upon it, and strengthening it in righteous-
ness by means of visions and divine locutions,
accompanied by a pure and singular sweetness,
whereby she was withdrawn from the desire of evil.

Mother de Saumaise wrote as follows : " I can say
that during the six years that I knew Sister Margaret
Mary Alacoque I never noticed any sluggishness in
her with respect to the resolution which she made on
the day when she consecrated herself to God by her
Religious profession of letting Him reign in her above
all and before all. She never allowed herself to in-
dulge in any satisfaction of mind or body. This
faithfulness drew down most special graces and
favours upon her from the Divine Goodness ; and
they led her to have a great desire for crosses,
humiliations, and sufferings, so much so that it
might be said without exaggeration that nobody
ever was more anxious for honours or pleasures
than she was for those, although whilst delighting
in them she felt them very keenly. Her wish to
be as like as possible to Jesus Christ made her do
and suffer with wonderful peace, patience, and sweetness much that was hard to human nature. When
she received any humiliation, contradiction, or mortification from anybody, she used to beg earnestly to
be allowed to inflict disciplines and other penances
upon herself for their sake ; for she was never so
happy as when she saw herself treated with contempt.
I shall not mention her exactness in all the duties of
the Religious life, and her severe and rigorous morti-

fications : I shall only mention that when she was mistress of the children, in order to overcome the feeling of disgust which she felt at the sight of an abscess in the foot of one of them, she put her mouth to it and sucked the rotten matter from it ; and she would have continued to do this had she not been forbidden. She did many other penances which were no less revolting to nature ; and she eagerly sought for them as soon as she learned that God had been offended. Jesus Christ one day spoke to her of the spiritual needs of a soul, and He desired her to give to Him whatever good she might do, and whatever sufferings might befal her, in order that this soul should obtain the graces needful for it. She at once sacrificed herself to His will, and soon afterwards fell ill, and also suffered great agony from a fall. She often thus suffered for the welfare of others, and she was always delighted to atone for offences committed against God."

CHAPTER VI.

ARGARET MARY was favoured with another vision of the Sacred Heart of Jesus Christ in the summer of the year 1674. " Jesus Christ, my sweet Master, showed Himself to me shining with glory one day during the Exposition of the Blessed Sacrament. His five wounds were brilliant like five suns, and flames burst forth on all sides from this sacred Humanity, but · especially from His adorable Breast ; and it opened and I beheld His most loving and beloved Heart, which was the living fountain of these flames. He then made known to me the unspeakable wonders of His pure love for men, and that He got only ingratitude from them. ' This ingratitude,' He said, ' wounded Me more than all else that I endured during My Passion. Yet all that I have endured for them would seem but little to My love, if only they would make some return to Me ; but they show. Me nothing save coldness, and they reject My endearments. Do thou at least give Me this pleasure

of making atonement for their ingratitude.' " [1]   Jesus
Christ then demanded two things from her, namely,
that she would receive Communion on the first Friday
of every month, and that she would rise from bed at
eleven o'clock every Thursday night and remain prostrate in prayer with her face to the earth for an hour,
in order to make atonement for all the sins of mankind, and in order to give consolation to His Heart
for this wholesale abandonment, of which the flight
of the Apostles in the Garden of Olives was but a
faint foreshadowing.

Margaret Mary was so overwhelmed by this wonderful vision that she swooned and lay speechless upon
the floor.   Some of the sisters finding her in that
state brought her to the mother superior, but she at
first could not utter a word.   When at length she
was able to speak she made known everything to her
superior ; and she sternly rebuked her and humiliated
her very much, but the lowly-minded nun bore it
patiently, and even rejoiced because she thought herself to be so wicked and worthless that the worst ill-
treatment would have seemed pleasant to her.   She
fell into a burning fever, but whilst her body was
torn with pain, her soul was flooded with spiritual
delight, and she thirsted for more suffering.   " This
burning fever was fed with the wood of the
cross alone, and with all sorts of contempt, humiliations, and afflictions, and I never felt any suffering so
much as that of not suffering enough." [1]   Her fever

[1] *Memoir.*

increased so much that she was thought to be dying, and the doctor was unable to help her. The mother superior then bade her beg Jesus Christ to restore her to health as a proof that her visions were from God. She prayed and the fever left her, and she was soon as well as she had ever been. Mother de Saumaise therefore allowed her to receive Communion on the first Friday of every month, and also to rise from bed every Thursday night in order to pray before the Blessed Sacrament. She was, nevertheless, bewildered at finding that a young nun, who was only two years in Religion, claimed to have such wonderful visions and revelations. She consulted some learned men in the town, but they at once declared that Margaret Mary was misled by her imagination, and perhaps even by the devil.

When Moses, by command of God, ascended Mount Nebo, he beheld the land of Chanaan, the land flowing with milk and honey which had been promised to his people, spread out beneath him towards the west, and he beheld its green meadows, bright vineyards, fair hills, flowing streams, and high-walled cities amid the plain ; but the people of Israel who were encamped at the foot of the mountain beheld only the dreary waste of brown sand around them. Margaret Mary likewise, having reached high holiness got a glimpse of the wonders of the heavenly country, and when she spoke of what she saw she was not believed, but was treated as a visionary.

Margaret Mary suffered very much on account of

her visions. Jesus Christ one day had shown her a large cross hidden beneath flowers, and had said to her, "This is the couch of My chaste spouses: these flowers shall fall little by little and only the thorns shall remain". She now lay forsaken and helpless upon her bed of prickly thorns. The mother superior began to distrust her, her confessor disbelieved her visions and revelations, and her sisters in Religion considered her as almost witless and treated her with contempt, found fault with her actions and devotions, and scolded her for her singularities; but she bore their mockery and railleries with meekness and good humour. She was more wonderful on account of her humble patience than on account of the great favours which God bestowed upon her. "Virtue," as Saint John of the Cross writes, "does not consist in thoughts and feelings about God, however sublime they may be, nor in any personal experience of this kind; but, on the contrary, in that which is not at all a matter of feeling—in great humility, contempt of self, and of all which belongs to self, deeply rooted in the soul, and in being glad that others should have the same opinion of us, and in not wishing to be esteemed by them. Visions, revelations, and heavenly feelings are notworthy the least act of humility." Margaret Mary showed the utmost respect to her fellow-Religious, obeyed them and humbled herself before them, and was always eager to do the lowliest household work, thus giving an evident proof that her supernatural favours came from God: for it is an evident sign that they are from God when they produce humility in the soul. She was even glad when she was slighted and made to suffer, for she once beheld the Sacred Heart as a garden, and heard these words, " Daughter, enter this delightful garden, and gather flowers at will "; but she said, " My Divine Love, I wish for nothing but Thee, who art a bundle of myrrh to me "; and Jesus Christ answered, " Thou hast chosen aright, for myrrh alone can preserve its perfume and beauty : this life is the time for it : there shall be none in eternity ".

Jesus Christ, however, was unwilling that the truth of her visions should any longer be doubted, and He sent the holy Jesuit Father de la Colombiere to Paray, towards the end of the year 1674, that he might witness in her favour, and might guide her safely along the dangerous pathway of religious perfection. Father de la Colombiere was endowed with great gifts both of nature and of grace, and was gifted with a personal experience of supernatural favours and great discernment of souls, and he led such a holy life that the process of his canonisation has been begun with the permission of the Holy See. He gave a spiritual conference to the nuns of the Visitation shortly after his arrival at Paray-le-Monial, and Margaret Mary heard a voice within her whilst he was speaking, which said these words : " This is he whom I send to you ". He came again to the convent to hear the confessions of the Religious during the Ember days of the following Lent, in the year 1675

and he came a few days afterwards in order to speak
with Margaret Mary about the state of her soul. She,
at the bidding of the mother superior, though with
great reluctance, made known everything fully and
clearly to him. "I laid bare my whole heart to him,
and showed to him the whole state of my soul, both
the good and the bad."[1] He acted with great prudence. He watched her very carefully, humbled her
much, often spoke harshly to her, and especially, tried
her obedience most severely. He acted in this way
for a long time, and, at length, clearly understood
that she was led by the spirit of God. He therefore
encouraged her, bade her not to fear but to follow
faithfully the guidance of the Lord. He, moreover,
said that she ought to thank God for His great goodness towards her, and to receive with reverence and
humility the familiar intercourse with which He
favoured her.

Margaret Mary faithfully followed the inspirations
sent to her by Jesus Christ. These divine sunbeams
quickened her soul and caused it to live, move, feel,
and work, according to the movements of His grace.
As when after the dark days and the bitter winds of
winter the warm breath of spring breathes new life
into nature, and the trees are richly clothed with green
foliage, and the meadows are golden with bright
blossoms, and the air is heavy with the sweet perfume
of flowers, so her beloved Spouse could say of her soul:
"The flowers have appeared in our land, the fig tree

[1] *Memoir.*

has put forth her green figs, the vines in flower yield
their sweet scent. Arise, My love, My beautiful one,
and come."[1] The love of God reigned as a queen in
her heart. She loved Him alone and above everything, and she loved everything else in Him and for
Him. The love of God was the life of her heart, and
she neither desired, feared, hoped for, or enjoyed
anything but Him. She took pleasure only in this
sweetest fruit of paradise, and it enabled her by its
sweetness to lead a holy life and to bear patiently
affronts, calumnies, and sufferings of every kind.
She, however, sometimes failed in her duties, for, as
Saint Francis of Sales writes, " As we see that good
trees never bring forth any hurtful fruit, yet sometimes
they bear green, unripe, or worm-eaten fruit, or
mistletoe or moss, so also great saints never commit
any mortal sin, but still they produce some useless,
immature, harsh, rough, and ill-favoured works ". She
was one day guilty of falling into a slight failing by
some little act of dissimulation when speaking, and at
another time she yielded somewhat to a feeling of
vanity, and she once showed a distaste for what she
had been told to do. But no sooner had she become
aware of her fault than she threw herself with the
utmost sorrow at the feet of Jesus Christ, and then
going to the reverend mother superior, humbly acknowledged it, and then earnestly entreated her to inflict
some very severe penance upon her in order that she
might make some atonement to her Divine Master.

[1] Canticle of Canticles, ii.

She was heartbroken with sorrow for her slightest failings, and she wondered that she was not annihilated by God for such sins. She would rather have suffered a thousand deaths than undergo the agony which she felt on coming before Him after having thus offended His holiness by any sinful action. "The anguish which I then endured made me feel as if I were in purgatory, and all within me was anguish, and anguish without any alleviation, so that I exclaimed in the bitterness of my soul : ' Oh, how awful a thing it is to fall into the hands of the living God '. I would willingly have thrown myself into any suffering rather than appear before the holiness of God with a single sin upon my soul." [1]

Margaret Mary was made assistant to the sister infirmarian, and she fulfilled this difficult office with great perfection. She then became assistant to the mistress of the children who were in the convent. Saint Francis of Sales would not allow the nuns of the Visitation to educate schoolgirls, but he allowed a few children who showed signs of a Religious vocation to stay with them, "for it is better," he said, "to have thorns with the roses in our garden, than to have no roses because of the thorns ". These children were called "sisters of the little habit". They wore a black dress with a short white veil, and were put under the care of a sister of great gentleness and prudence. Margaret Mary fulfilled her new duties with the utmost enactness and perfection, and taught the young

[1] *Memoir.*

girls to love God and to lead a holy life. When she
joined with them in their games and amusements she
was wont to speak to them of holy things, and she
spoke to them so sweetly that they were never weary
of listening to her. She corrected their faults with
great gentleness, but chastised them severely whenever
they were guilty of falsehood or particular friendship.
She sought by prayer and penance to sanctify them,
and she was wont to pour out long and fervent
prayers for them before the Blessed Sacrament, entreating the Lord most earnestly to bestow His best
gifts upon them and preserve them from every sin.
She also offered up her Communions and other
spiritual exercises for their welfare.

Margaret Mary once suffered exquisite pain from a
whitlow which had grown upon her hand, and as she
was unable to sleep she sat at the fireside in the
dormitory of the children during the weary hours of
the night, carefully abstaining from disturbing them.
One of them, however, saw her, and told the
mother superior about it, and she asked Margaret
Mary why she had not made it known, but she
answered, "Dear mother, it was so trifling a thing
that I did not think that it was worth while men-
tioning it". The surgeon found it so deep-seated and
dangerous that he cut it out even to the bone, and
when he saw her bear the frightful pain so patiently,
he could not help saying, "It is very good to be holy,
for it makes us insensible to pain". She bore not
only physical pain but mental pain with the utmost

meekness and patience, for when her sisters in Religion sometimes thoughtlessly made fun of her, or called her a hypocrite, a silly creature, a whimsical woman, she gave no heed to their jests and mockery, and always spoke kindly and graciously to them. A school-girl one day having overheard them laughing and scoffing at her, said to her, "Mother, you are very good to bear all this," but she merely answered, "My child, let us go before the Blessed Sacrament and ask forgiveness for our faults, and we shall also pray for those who have given to me this opportunity of suffering somewhat for Jesus Christ".

CHAPTER VII.

ESUS CHRIST granted to Margaret Mary another inward vision of His Sacred Heart in reward for her wonderful humility, purity, and patience. He showed His Sacred Heart to her one day during the Octave of the Feast of Corpus Christi, in the month of June, 1675, as she knelt in prayer before the Blessed Sacrament, and He said in the depths of her soul: "Behold this Heart which has loved men so much that It has left nothing undone, exhausting and consuming Itself in order to prove to them Its love; and I receive in return from most men only ingratitude by their disrespect and sacrileges, and by the coldness and contempt which they show to Me in this Sacrament of love; and what I feel most keenly is that these are hearts which are consecrated to Me. I therefore demand that the first Friday after the Octave of Corpus Christi be made a special festival in honour of My Sacred Heart, by receiving Communion on that day, and by making a reparation of honour in

atonement for the insults which are offered to It : and
I promise that My Heart shall open wide to pour out
plentifully the influences of Its love upon all those
who shall give such honour to It, or cause it to be
given."[1] These words gave her a burning thirst to
suffer for the Sacred Heart : to receive It in Communion, and to make satisfaction to It for the insults
which It so often received from men. She was filled
to overflowing with love for that Sacred Heart which
loved men so much, and was overwhelmed with
sorrow because a Heart which was so holy, so
lovely, and so worthy of love was despised and ill-
treated by them.

Margaret Mary gave a full account by word of
mouth, and in writing, of the wonderful vision which
had been given to her by Jesus Christ, to the director
of her soul, Father de la Colombiere. He carefully
examined it, and after much prayer declared it to be
the work of God. He consecrated himself to the
Sacred Heart on the following Friday, June 21, and
he received so great an abundance of grace, and such
an outflow of the love of God, that he was still more
persuaded of the truth of the revelation, and he
thenceforth worked unceasingly to spread the devotion
of the Sacred Heart amongst the inhabitants of Paray.
Many were converted by it, and many more by its
means went forward rapidly upon the road of spiritual
perfection. He at this time wrote the following letter
to his sister, who was a Visitation nun at Condrien :

[1] *Memoir.*

" I entreat you to receive Communion on the Friday
after the Octave of Corpus Christi, in order to make
atonement for the insults offered to our Lord. This
custom has been recommended by a person of
wonderful holiness, who declares that the greatest
blessings shall come to those who give this token of
love to our Lord. Try to win over your friends to
the practice of a like devotion."

The mother superior, who daily witnessed her great
humility, obedience, and love of suffering, believed
that her visions were true, and that she was led by the
spirit of God, but she nevertheless slighted and scolded
her as if they were merely the result of a disturbed
imagination ; she, however, allowed her to perform the
acts of devotion which had been recommended to her
by Jesus Christ. Her sisters in Religion did not
understand her extraordinary ways, and thought that
she was misled by the devil, and the reverend
mother, wishing to keep her humble, did not un-
deceive them. Some amongst them looked upon her
as possessed, or, at least, as obsessed by the evil spirit,
and they sometimes threw holy water upon her, and
made the sign of the cross over her, in order to drive
away the devil. They even strove to turn her holy
director against her, and they endeavoured to persuade him that she was deceiving him, but he
continued to help and console her, although he was
not sparing in humiliations and mortifications.
Father de la Colombiere was sent by his superiors
shortly afterwards to London. He gave testimony to

her holiness before he set out, and when he arrived in London he practised and preached the devotion of the Sacred Heart with still greater zeal than before. He got Margaret Mary's written account of her vision printed, and in the year 1677 he wrote as follows to a friend in France: "I know that God wishes me to serve Him by obtaining the fulfilment of His desires regarding the devotion which He has made known to a person to whom He speaks very familiarly. I have taught it already to many persons in England, and I have written to France about this devotion, and asked one of my friends to spread it in his neighbourhood: it will do a great deal of good there."

Very great crosses of every kind are sent by God, according to the teaching of Saint Teresa, to all those upon whom He bestows wonderful favours; and when Saint Paul was taken up to the third heavens there was given to him a sting of the flesh, an angel of Satan, to buffet him. Margaret Mary was likewise afflicted by many outward and inward tribulations, and a great storm of temptation burst upon her. The evil spirit breathed with his loathsome breath upon her, and her mind was filled with thoughts of vanity, gluttony, hatred, pride, and despondency. She was especially very strongly tempted to gluttony, and had always an insatiable craving for food except when she sat down to her meals. Her life became thenceforward a constant warfare against the evil suggestions of the devil, but she never grew weary of praying to God for help, humbled herself under His powerful Hand, and always made known her temptations to the mother superior. And thus she never yielded to them; for "no evils shall happen to him that fears the Lord, but in temptation God will keep him : a wise man hates not the commandments and justices, and he shall not be dashed to pieces as a ship in a storm ".[1] She stood steadfast like a rock amid the mighty waves of the sea which gather and dash over it with a great roar, seeming as if they would shatter it ; but when they have broken themselves thereon, it still stands shining in the sunlight, with snow-white wreaths of foam glittering upon its smooth surface.

God at the same time allowed her soul to be overshadowed with a thick darkness, and every thought of her mind and every feeling of her heart seemed to her to be so many sins. She no longer had sweet delights when praying; she felt no sensible consciousness of loving God; her religious duties became irksome to her ; she looked upon herself as misled by the devil and forsaken by God, and her onward progress was made, not amid sunshine and song, but amid coldness and gloom. Although she no longer felt any pleasure in prayer or the exercises of holy love, but was overwhelmed with dryness of spirit, scruples, temptations, and fears about her salvation, she, nevertheless, faithfully fulfilled all her religious duties, practised all her usual penances, kept stainless from the slightest

---

[1] Ecclesiasticus xxxiii.

sin, and served God with as much fidelity as when He
filled her soul with spiritual sweetness. She watched
and fought with unconquerable courage, heedless of
the shouts and threats of the foe, and by this strife
her soul became more pleasing and more closely
united to God; for as flowers when they are crushed
give forth a more delicious fragrance, so her virtues
became more perfect in infirmity and more pleasing to
the Sacred Heart of Jesus Christ. Her good works
and acts of love gave great pleasure to God, although
they gave no pleasure to herself, and she was like a
sweet singer who, being deaf, nevertheless gives
delight to those who listen to him. "One of the
best musicians in the world," writes Saint Francis of
Sales, "who played perfectly on the lute, became in
time so very deaf as to lose altogether the sense of
hearing, but he did not, nevertheless, cease to sing
and to handle his lute with wonderful delicacy of
touch through his great skill, which his deafness did
not take from him. However, as he had no pleasure
in his song nor yet in the sound of his lute, inasmuch
as, being without his hearing, he was not able to perceive its sweetness and beauty, he no longer sang or
played save only to give pleasure to a prince, whose
subject he was and whom he was most strongly
moved, as well as strongly bound, to please, since he
had been brought up from childhood in his palace.
He, therefore, took the greatest delight in pleasing
him, and when his prince showed that he was pleased
with his music he was ravished with gladness. It

sometimes happened, however, that the prince, in order
to make trial of this loving musician's love, gave him a
command to sing, and then immediately leaving him
there in his chamber, went to the chase. The desire
which this singer had to fulfill his master's will made
him continue his music as attentively as if his prince
were present, although, indeed, he had no pleasure in
in singing, for he had neither the pleasure of the
melody of which his deafness deprived him, nor the
satisfaction of giving pleasure to his prince, who, being
absent, could not enjoy the sweetness of the beautiful
airs which he sang." Margaret Mary likewise gave
very great pleasure to Jesus Christ by her faithfulness
amidst that storm of temptation and of aridity of soul.
And as when the storm blows the ship flies swiftly
onwards through the foaming billows towards the
peaceful harbour, so her soul then made rapid progress on the way of perfection. She, however, at the
bidding of the mother superior, who was bewildered
at her state, prayed to Jesus Christ to still the storm,
and He heard her prayer, and peace once more took
possession of her heart.

Margaret Mary got a visit one day from her brother
and his wife, and she as usual spoke of holy things.
Her sister-in-law, who hitherto had led a somewhat
worldly life, began to weep, and her husband scolded
her, but Margaret Mary said, " Let her weep, for
these tears are good ". He went away, leaving them
together, and his holy sister said to the weeping
woman, " Why do you weep : can I do anything

for you ? "　" Yes, you can," answered the lady ; and
when Margaret Mary asked her how she might assist
her, the other answered, " By praying to God for my
salvation ".　" I will pray to God for your salvation as
if I were praying for my own," said the holy nun,
" but God makes known to me that it will cost you
dear."　" No matter," answered the lady ; " I submit
entirely to His will."　When, a few hours later, her
husband returned, Margaret Mary told him what had
happened, and promised to make a novena for his
wife.　" Both of you," she said, " will need patience :
pray therefore to God for it."　He was frightened
when he heard these words, for he was very fond of
her.　A few days after their return home to Bois
Sainte Marie, his wife suddenly felt a most severe
pain in her head and face, which thenceforth caused
her such agony that she uttered shrieks both day and
night.　The most skilful doctors of the town and of
Lyons, whither he took her, were utterly unable to
give her the slightest relief ; and he then wrote a
most piteous appeal for help to his holy sister at
Paray, but she answered that the only remedy was
the utmost patience and resignation to the will of
God.　At the end of a year he once more wrote
entreating her to pray to God for the restoration to
health of his beloved wife, and she wrote the following letter in answer :

　" Indeed, my dear brother, I do not know what
more I can say to you ; I am deeply grieved to see
that all the prayers which our community and other

excellent souls of my acquaintance unite in offering up for my dear sister and for yourself have not succeeded in obtaining for you a moment's patience : this I attribute to my sins. Yet this is what God desires from both of you : resignation to His will and patience to bear sweetly this trial, and not to allow yourself to have recourse to those things which are not pleasing to Him. I thought that I had said enough in the two former letters, if you had reflected upon it, to make you perceive that since it is the will of God that she should suffer this pain for her salvation, it is idle to seek human remedies for it, because they will be useless ; for who can gainsay the will of God, which is always fulfilled whether we wish it or not. To speak plainly, the salvation of the soul of this poor sufferer depends upon this pain and upon the good or bad use which she makes of it ; and she ought not to wish even to know whether it will last for a long or a short time ; let her leave it to God, to whom she should sacrifice her life, in order to give it back to Him whenever He shall be pleased to take it. I most earnestly entreat you with tears in my eyes to follow this advice, for I know that God has sent this illness to her as a mark of His love and desire to save her, and that He could not give her a stronger proof of His anger than by restoring her to health. When salvation is at stake we must do everything, suffer everything, sacrifice and forsake everything.

" This, my dear brother, is what my lively sorrow and my share in your affliction allows me to say to you. As for prayers, it seems to me that I cannot do more for you. Our much-honoured mother has had many novenas made for this purpose, and is much concerned for your affliction. As for myself, I cannot express the surprise which I feel at your want of resignation and patience, and it gives me the utmost pain. Make another vow on her behalf to Saint Francis of Sales ; get nine Masses said in order to obtain patience for her and detachment from worldly things. Let her remember that the last time I saw her she begged me to pray to God for her salvation, no matter what it might cost her ; and it is too late now to recall it. But, my dear brother, although God desires to save us, it is His will that we should contribute our share towards it, otherwise He will do nothing ;. we must, therefore, make up our minds to suffer. Now is the time for a fruitful sowing for eternity, where the harvest shall be abundant. Do not lose courage : trials borne patiently are worth a thousand times more than any other austerity ; and it is this which God now requires of you. I embrace the dear invalid a thousand times."

Margaret Mary wrote again shortly afterwards, and warned them that the suffering woman would not be freed from her pain until she became wholly resigned to the will of God. She at length yielded to the entreaties of Margaret Mary : gave up all human remedies, resolved to bear her illness in future with patience, offered up her sufferings for her salvation, threw herself entirely into the hands of God, and

resigned herself to His holy will. God was well
pleased with her sacrifice, and the following day
she was freed for ever from her sufferings by a holy
and happy death.

CHAPTER VIII.

OTHER DE SAUMAISE ceased to be mother superior of the Visitation Convent at Paray in the year 1678, and Mother Greyfié became superior in her stead. Mother Greyfié had entered the Visitation Convent at Annecy, the fountainhead of the Order, when she was a child, and had been educated by some of the first companions of Saint Jane de Chantal. She made her vows when she was fifteen years of age, and lived for many years under the spiritual guidance of the wise and holy Mother de Chaugy. She became very enlightened in the way of perfection, and had so great a love for the Rules of the Order that she was called " a living Rule ". When she left Annecy, the mother superior wrote to the nuns at Paray that it was a great sacrifice to lose her; that she was very well suited to govern, as she was very firm, mild, humble, straightforward, and very exact in regular observance. She found when she came to Paray that the nuns of that convent were holy and pious; but she soon saw that they were much divided in opinion about

Margaret Mary, and that, whilst a few revered her as a saint, most of them, and especially those who were most strict in the observance of the Rule, looked upon her as misled either by her imagination or by the devil.

Mother Greyfié was gifted in a special way with the discernment of spirits, and had a great distrust of extraordinary ways in the Religious life; and she therefore endeavoured to find out the truth whether she was led by a good or by an evil spirit, by constantly humbling her, trying her obedience, and inflicting very severe penances upon her. She mortified her in every way at all times, bidding her give up her favourite devotions, publicly blaming her and punishing her severely for the least faults, and privately refusing her permission to perform the penances of her own choice, but giving her instead other penances more painful and humbling. She seemed to disbelieve her supernatural favours, and spoke of them with contempt. Margaret Mary bore this for three years with child-like simplicity and docility, and always blindly obeyed her, told her freely and frankly all that happened in her soul, and trusted in her and loved her as a mother. Mother Greyfié afterwards wrote the following account of her conduct at that time : "When I entered on the service of your house, although your community was very good and full of holiness and piety, I nevertheless found opinions very much divided about this true spouse of the crucified Saviour. I, therefore, hardly ever gave any signs of belief in the wonderful things that took place in her, in order to keep every sister in peace and quiet. I allowed others to blame her whenever she did anything that was displeasing, and I blamed her myself if it was done in my presence, even when she acted by my orders or with my permission. She, nevertheless, always thought herself guilty, and she was always asking for penances, in order to satisfy the divine justice."

Her temptations continued to afflict her, and she was sometimes overwhelmed with the thought that she had no right to hope for heaven, since she was without the love of God, and this thought often made her weep bitterly. She sometimes felt a very great hunger, especially when praying, and that was a frightful torture. "My mother superior, from whom I hid nothing that happened within me, bade me come and ask for something to eat whenever I felt a great attack of hunger. I did it with the utmost dislike, on account of the great shame which I felt when doing it; but she, instead of sending me to take something to eat, mortified and humbled me very much, telling me to keep my hunger, and that I might satisfy it when the rest of the community went to the refectory. I then remained at peace in my suffering."[1] The mother superior knew that this unnatural appetite was a temptation of the devil, and she therefore told her to bear her hunger with patience, and to humble herself before God at the thought of her temptation,

[1] *Memoir.*

hoping firmly in His grace and help. Margaret Mary suffered also at the same time from a parching thirst, and nevertheless she spent fifty days without drinking anything, in order to honour the burning thirst of our Lord upon the cross, as well as to honour the burning thirst of His Sacred Heart for the salvation of sinners. She was not satisfied with this very severe penance, but she also abstained from drinking either water or wine every week from Thursday until Saturday, until she was at length forbidden by the mother superior to practise this mortification. When the mother superior bade her satisfy her thirst she obeyed, but she drank only the water with which the plates and dishes had been washed. The mother superior having learned this, scolded her sharply for it, saying, in the words of their holy founder, "True obedience obeys not only the command, but also the intention, of the superior".

Margaret Mary had cut the holy name of Jesus on her breast, and when the letters were, in course of time, effaced, she renewed them with a lighted taper. When the mother superior bade her show the wound to the sister infirmarian, she prayed to Jesus Christ to heal her, and her petition was granted; but the mother superior, in punishment of her unwillingness, deprived her of Holy Communion. Her greatest sorrow, however, was for having displeased her sovereign Master by her want of blind obedience.

Margaret Mary had an accident at this time which caused her much suffering. "I remember," writes

Mother Greyfié, "that one day whilst she was drawing water, the bucket which she had just filled fell from her hands, and as it fell back into the well, the iron handle of the windlass struck her on the face so violently that it broke her teeth and also a bit of her gum of about the size and thickness of half a finger. She gave no heed to it beyond begging one of the children, whose mistress she then was, to cut away the piece of flesh which still adhered. The children, however, were frightened at seeing her in such a plight and would not touch it. She therefore cut it away herself as well as she could with the help of her scissors; but the wound in her mouth gave her great pain as often as she had to take food. The blow also gave her a pain in the temples which, after every meal, became almost unbearable, like a very violent toothache. The only relief she sought was to go, with permission, from the recreation, and walk in the garden until the pain had become less. She then rejoined the others. She bore all these sufferings without complaining and without even asking for any relief."

Margaret Mary indeed loved sufferings, and had chosen a suffering life rather than a life of pleasure and earthly happiness, for Jesus Christ had enlightened her to know the great worth of humiliations and sufferings, and He had allowed her to choose between a life of pleasure and a life of suffering. He one day showed her as it were a picture of a very happy life, a life of peace and inward and outward consolation, together with the best health and the approbation and esteem of all; and also a picture of a poor and lowly life, a life of humiliation, contempt, and contradiction; and He bade her choose between them, promising to give her the same graces whichever she chose. But she begged Him to choose for her, saying to Him that He was sufficient for her, and that she wished for nothing save His greater glory. Jesus Christ then made known to her that she, like Mary Magdalen, had chosen the better part, and that he would be her inheritance for ever; and He chose for her a life of suffering, saying, "This is what I have chosen for you, for it gives most pleasure to Me, both for the fulfilment of My designs and to make you like unto Me. The other is a life of enjoyment and not of merit, and is kept for heaven." She shuddered at the prospect before her of years of suffering and of humiliation; but her love for Jesus Christ was so strong, and she lived so much more in Him than in herself that she conformed to His wishes and His good pleasure, and bravely took up the cross which He laid upon her, and drank eagerly the bitter chalice which He offered to her.

Margaret Mary had made known to Mother Greyfié what Jesus Christ had inspired her to do in honour of His Sacred Heart. "I remember that the first time I had the happiness of speaking with this dear sister," wrote Mother Greyfié, "she seemed to me to have a strong and burning desire to find out some way of making this adorable Heart known, loved, and adored, if possible, by the whole world. She was held back, however, by the lowly opinion which she had of herself, and this became greater every day. She thought that it was enough for her to share in the work in order to spoil it, and to give others a dislike for the devotion of which she was so fond, and to spread which she would willingly have sacrificed a thousand lives." Margaret Mary told her also about her practice of praying every Thursday night prostrate on the ground in obedience to the wish of Jesus Christ, in order to honour His Sacred Heart, and to make atonement for the ungratefulness of men ; but Mother Greyfié forbade her to continue that devout practice. Margaret Mary blindly obeyed her mother superior, for she knew that according to the teaching of Saint Francis of Sales, God guides souls through obedience, and that everything which is done outside obedience is a deception. " When God puts inspirations into a heart, the first which He gives is obedience. Was there ever a more clear and unmistakeable inspiration than that which was given to the glorious Saint Paul. And the chief point of it was that he should go to the city where he should learn what he was to do from the mouth of Ananias ; and this Ananias, a very famous man, was, as Saint Dorotheus writes, the Bishop of Damascus. Whoever says he is inspired, and yet will not obey his superiors and follow their advice is an impostor." [1]

Margaret Mary well understood this wise teaching

---

[1] *Love of God*, viii. 13.

of Saint Francis and acted upon it. However, whilst she was praying one day, Jesus Christ made known to her that He was displeased at the ceasing of these devotional practices in honour of His Sacred Heart; and she told this to Mother Greyfié, saying that she feared that God would send some affliction as a punishment. A young nun, who was fondly loved and was highly esteemed by Mother Greyfié, died suddenly soon afterwards, and the circumstances of her death were of such a kind that Mother Greyfié was convinced that her death was a judgment of God upon herself for her disbelief. She, therefore, no longer withheld from Margaret Mary permission to practise her special devotions in honour of the Sacred Heart. But she soon afterwards fell into her former doubts, both because she was distrustful of extra-ordinary ways, and because she was very much worried by the nuns, who never ceased complaining of the singularities of Margaret Mary. She was somewhat freed, however, from her misgivings by a miracle that happened on the Feast of Corpus Christi, in the year 1680. She had gone into the infirmary on the eve of the feast to visit Margaret Mary, who was only beginning to recover from a very severe illness: and when she was leaving Margaret Mary asked her to allow her to get up the next morning in order to hear Holy Mass. Margaret Mary, seeing that she hesitated to give permission, said to her in a winning way, "My dear mother, if you wish it, our Lord also will wish it, and will give me strength". Mother

Greyfié then bade the sister infirmarian give her something to eat the following morning, and then help her
to get up and go to hear Holy Mass. Margaret Mary,
feeling much better towards evening, begged the
sister infirmarian to get permission for her to get up
fasting in order that she might have the happiness of
receiving Communion on the feast. The sister
infirmarian forgot to do so, but as soon as she had
helped her to get up the next morning, she thought of
it, and went in haste to seek the mother superior.
As she was going out of the infirmary by one door
the mother superior came in by another door, and
when she saw Margaret Mary out of bed, and found
that she was still fasting, she rebuked her severely,
saying that she was acting through self-will and
through want of obedience, submission, and simplicity. She then bade her go to Mass and to
Communion, but that as self-will had given her so
much strength and courage, she should take her bed-
clothes to her cell and go to the choir when the bell
rang, and follow the community exercises for the
next five months without going back again to the
infirmary. Margaret Mary received this rebuke on
her knees, with her hands joined, and with a calm
and meek look, and she then humbly begged forgiveness and penance for her fault. Mother Greyfié, as
soon as Margaret Mary had left the infirmary, went to
her room and wrote as follows : " I, the undersigned,
by the power given to me by God as superior over
Sister Margaret Mary, order her, in virtue of holy

obedience, to ask our Lord, with such fervour and earnestness to give her health, as may move His goodness to grant it to her in order not to be always a burden to holy Religion, and in order to be able to practise always the community exercises, and this until the Presentation of our Lady of this year 1680, on which day we shall see what has to be done for the future.—Sister Peronne-Rosalie Greyfié, Superior." Margaret Mary had no sooner got this obedience than she was entirely healed and restored to unwonted health. "At the time of the Elevation of the Holy Mass I felt sensibly that all my sickness was taken away, like the taking off a dress, and I found that I had the strength and health of a very healthy person who had never been sick."[1] All the nuns were filled with wonder at this great miracle, and the mother superior considered it to be a strong proof that all her extraordinary ways were the work of God. She thenceforth followed the community exercises, and did household work like the rest, and during the five following months had excellent health, but at the end of five months she fell back into her former ill-health. Mother Greyfié wrote to her the following declaration, May 25 : "I hereby declare that I have witnessed that state of health in you which I ordered you to ask our Lord to give to you, and I must acknowledge, therefore, that what has happened and still takes place in your soul comes from the incomprehensible goodness and mercy of the Sacred Heart of Jesus. I

[1] *Memoir.*

believe it; but I command you to pray again to God the Father, through our Lord Jesus Christ, to continue your health to you for a whole year, from the time of the first obedience which you received, out of love for Him, and to free me still further from every doubt." Margaret Mary recovered her health as soon as she had got this new obedience, and remained in good health for a twelvemonth. The mother superior was told by one of the nuns, who had witnessed this miracle, that she "ought to order Sister Margaret Mary not to return to the infirmary for two years since she had succeeded so well"; but the wise superior answered: "That is sufficient to convince me that our sister is guided by God".

CHAPTER IX.

ATHER DE LA COLOMBIERE, who was living in the palace of the Duke of York, at London, was seized about midnight in his bedroom, November, 1678, and was thrown into prison, and, after having been kept there for three weeks, was banished for ever from the kingdom for the crime of having converted many to the Catholic faith, and of having helped to send an Irish priest to preach the Gospel to the people of Virginia in North America. He arrived at Paris in the beginning of January, 1679, and by command of his superior set out soon afterwards for Lyons. He passed through Paray on his way there, and he was enthusiastically welcomed as a martyr by the inhabitants. He laboured much for their spiritual welfare during the ten days of his stay, although he was worn out by his unceasing work for the salvation of souls and by the hardships of his imprisonment. He went frequently to visit the monastery of the Visitation, and after a long conversation one day with Margaret Mary, he said to the mother superior that he was certain that all that happened in the soul of

that dear sister came from God, as there was no mark of delusion in it, since humility, simplicity, obedience, and mortification are not fruits of the spirit of darkness, and these words gave great comfort to her. He also wrote to Mother de Saumaise, who was then at Dijon : " I saw Sister Margaret Mary only once, but I was much consoled by the visit. I found her extremely humble and obedient, with a great love of the cross and of humiliations. These are signs of the Spirit that guides her, and they have never misled anyone." Father de la Colombiere stayed at Lyons for two years and a half, leading there a very holy life and doing very great good by word and example. He came back to Paray in the month of August of the year 1681, and spent the last six months of his life in that town. He did his best whilst he dwelt there to spread devotion to the Sacred Heart, teaching his penitents to practise the devotions of the "holy hour," of receiving Communion on the first Friday of each month, and of setting apart the Friday after the Octave of Corpus Christi as a special feast day in honour of the Sacred Heart of Jesus Christ, "having learned from a very holy soul that very special graces were given to those who faithfully practised these devotions". He died a holy death, February 15, in the year 1682.

Margaret Mary was not sorrowful at his death, for she knew that he was a saint. Mother Greyfié wrote afterwards : " I never noticed that she was sorry for him, but I often heard her express her joy at the

thought of his everlasting happiness, and thank the
Sacred Heart of Jesus Christ for all the graces which He
had bestowed on this worthy Religious both during
his life and at his death". God made known to her
the great heavenly glory of His servant, for she one
day beheld the Sacred Heart sending forth bright
beams from a flaming throne placed on a lofty and
beautiful eminence. The Blessed Virgin was there
together with Saint Francis of Sales and Father de la
Colombiere, and the Blessed Virgin told her that the
Visitation Order was the foremost possessor and
sanctuary of the Sacred Heart of her Divine Son, and
turning to Father de la Colombiere, she said sweetly :
"Faithful servant of my Divine Son, thou hast a great
share in this precious treasure, for if it is the privilege
of the daughters of the Visitation to make It known
and loved, it is for the fathers of thy society to make
known Its utility and worth ; and according as they
give this pleasure to It, this Divine Heart, the fruitful
fountain of blessings and graces, will plentifully fructify
their apostolic labours, so that they shall bear fruit
beyond their toil and hopes, and shall also be for
their own salvation and perfection".

Margaret Mary received about this time another
wonderful favour from the Sacred Heart of Jesus
Christ. She writes as follows : " I withdrew one day
during worktime into a small court near the Blessed
Sacrament, and whilst I was working there on my
knees, I felt myself inwardly and outwardly absorbed.
I then beheld the amiable Heart of my adorable Jesus

8

shining more brightly than the sun. It seemed to be amidst flames, and these flames were those of His love. It was surrounded by seraphim, who, with surpassing harmony, sang these words: 'Love triumphs. Love is rewarded. Love rejoices.' Then the blessed spirits invited me to join them in their hymn of praise to the Sacred Heart of Jesus Christ. I dared not do it, but they rebuked me, saying that they had come in order to join me in offering an unceasing homage of love, adoration, and praise to this Sacred Heart; that they would for this purpose take my place before the Blessed Sacrament in order that I might be able through means of them to love without interruption, and that they would have a share in the love which made me suffer, as I should share through them in their joyful love. It seemed to me as if they wrote this agreement in golden letters on the Sacred Heart in unfading letters of love. This communication lasted for about two or three hours. I have felt the effects of it during my whole lifetime as well by the help which I have received from this union as by the sweetness which it has caused and still causes in me. I was overwhelmed with shame, nevertheless, when, speaking with these holy angels, I called them my divine associates. This favour gave me so great a yearning to have purity of intention, and so high an idea of what was needful in order to speak with God that everything seemed to me to be foul in comparison with the fervour of the seraphim."[1]

[1] *Memoir.*

Jesus Christ, having allowed her soul thus to get a glimpse of the glory of His Sacred Heart, again withdrew His sweetness from her, and she fell once more into very great dryness and desolation of spirit, but she did not lose courage or grow weary of her prayers and penances. "Many imagine," writes Saint John of the Cross, "that the whole business of prayer consists in sensible devotion, and they strive to obtain it with all their might, wearying their brains and disturbing all the powers of their soul. When they are without that sensible devotion they become downcast, thinking they have done nothing. This effort to obtain sweetness destroys true devotion and spirituality, which consists in perseverance in prayer with patience and humility ; mistrustful of oneself, and seeking to please God alone. And, therefore, when they once miss their usual sweetness in prayer they feel a sort of repugnance to resume it, and sometimes give it up entirely." Margaret Mary was not guilty of this folly, and did not become less fervent during these weary days of desolation, for she loved God more than she loved herself. She clung fast to the Cross, which is a tree of life to those who lay hold of it when they are buffeted by the billows of tribulation, and this time of spiritual desolation became for her a seedtime which was followed by a plentiful harvest. She loved the Crucified, and entered therefore during the time of desolation into a closer union with God in the interior of her heart, for "there is nothing which causes such an earnest search for God as desolation ; nor is

there anything which so much draws God to the
heart as desolation, for acts of uniformity to the
divine will which are made during desolation are
purer and more perfect than any others; and therefore the greater the desolation the greater is the
humility, the purer are the prayers, and the more
plentiful are the divine graces and helps ". [1]

Margaret Mary had a burning love for Jesus Christ
in the Blessed Sacrament, for sufferings and for death.
" He has put in my soul three persecutors that torment
me continually. The first, which produces the two
others, is so great a desire of loving Him that I would
wish to see everything changed into flames of love in
order that He might be loved in the Adorable Sacrament. I feel constantly urged to suffer, whilst I feel
at the same time a terrible repugnance for suffering in
the lower part of my soul, and this makes my crosses
so heavy and painful that I would have sunk beneath
them, only that the Adorable Heart of my Jesus
strengthened and helped me in all my wants. My
soul also suffers the utmost agony at not yet being
able to leave my body. The greatest sacrifice which
I can make is that of still continuing to live. I, however, accept even this until doomsday if my God so
wills it, although the thought of being separated from
my Sovereign Good is worse than a thousand deaths." [2]

Margaret Mary learned from Jesus Christ to love
His holy Mother, to set great value on the Holy Mass,
and to desire ardently to receive Him in Holy Com-

[1] St. Alphonsus Liguori.　　[2] *Memoir.*

munion. She had always since her childhood had a wonderful love for the Blessed Virgin Mary, and she loved her daily more and more, and the Blessed Virgin watched over her with the fond affection of a mother. She broke forth into rapturous words of love, praise, and thanksgiving, when she remembered how God, whose throne is heaven, whose footstool is the earth, who is seated in inaccessible light, surrounded by myriads of bright angels, who ever bow down with lowliest worship before Him, had sent one of the seven chief Spirits of that mighty throng to her cottage at Nazareth to salute her as the mother of His only-begotten Son ; how He had filled her sinless soul to overflowing with the riches of His heavenly graces in order that she might be the worthy mother of so great a Son ; how the Redeemer promised to the patriarchs and foretold by the prophets had dwelt in her immaculate womb, had been fondled in her arms and fed at her breasts ; how through her a new creation had been made upon earth, a new day had dawned upon its darkness, and the world, lost by the sin of Eve, had been restored to its former happy state : how she had been chosen to crush the serpent's head, and is now seated at the right hand of her Divine Son as the Queen of heaven. She therefore kept her festival days with great devotion, said the Rosary, as well as many other prayers, fasted frequently in her honour, fled to her for help whenever she was tempted to sin, and eagerly strove to win her love by carefully imitating her virtues.

Margaret Mary also loved to hear the Holy Mass,
for she well knew that nothing gives such great glory
to God, that nothing so satisfies for sin, and that
nothing so merits His favours as this wonderful
sacrifice which ever renews the work of redemption.
She often offered to God praise and thanksgiving,
and the tribute of an humble and contrite heart ;
but she preferred to offer up to Him with the priest
His own Divine Son. She knew that from the day
that He made heaven and earth, and bade the newly-
made earth bear green herbs and shrubs and trees,
and the sea bring forth creeping things having life,
the heavens have proclaimed His greatness, and day
has passed on the praise to day, and night has taken
up the burden of the song ! But she knew that
neither the enduring music of nature nor the daily
sacrifices of sheep and unspotted oxen, nor the ever
up-going prayers of holy men, nor even the world-
renowned sacrifice of an only son by the hoary
patriarch of the Jewish people, gave sufficient glory
to God and thanksgiving for His benefits ; and that,
therefore, His only-begotten Son became man and
lay a little Babe upon the straw at Bethlehem, whilst
the angels sang " Glory to God in the highest ".
She also knew that neither Jesus' sighs nor tears, nor
yet His weary wanderings through Judea and Galilee,
when He dwelt upon earth, gave such great glory to
God as His death upon the cross at Calvary ; and
that His death, in obedience to His Father's will,
was the voice of praise most sweet to His Heavenly

Father's ear; and she well knew that this infinite
Sacrifice of praise, propitiation, adoration, and thanksgiving was offered up anew whenever the holy sacrifice
of the Mass was offered up by the priest upon the
altar. She therefore failed not to hear as many
Masses as she was able; and whilst the Holy Mass
was being said she seemed to be standing with the
holy women at the foot of the cross on Calvary.

She had a great yearning for Holy Communion.
She said to the mother superior: "I have so great
a desire to receive Communion that were it necessary
to walk barefoot through the flames I think that the
pain would be nothing in comparison with what I
would feel if I were deprived of so great a good.
Nothing can give me such gladness as this Bread of
Life. I remain annihilated, as it were, before my
God when I have received it; and I have a joy that
ravishes my whole being, so that I am inwardly in the
deepest silence for half a quarter of an hour listening
to the voice of Him who is the delight and satisfaction
of my soul."[1] Margaret Mary knew that the Blessed
Eucharist was the living Bread that came down from
heaven to give everlasting life to the souls of men,
and therefore the eve of Communion-day was a happy
time for her; and she spent nearly the whole night
speaking lovingly to Jesus Christ, whose flesh and
blood she was about to receive. As soon as she
had eaten of that heavenly food she overflowed with
tender love and thankfulness, and uttered sighs of

[1] *Memoir.*

loving affection. "O love! O the excess of the love of God to such a wretched creature!" The thought that men were so wicked as to receive the Bread of Life unworthily filled her mind with horror; and she once in vision saw these men binding Jesus Christ with ropes, and trampling upon Him; and she heard Him say: "Behold how sinners ill-treat Me". She received Communion very frequently; and the mother superior, when any nun was absent, made her communicate in her stead. Her great yearning after Holy Communion made her carefully watch over herself in order to lead a sinless life, that she might be worthy to receive Jesus Christ into her soul. She therefore seldom joined in conversation, and she always strove to induce her sisters to speak of God and of spiritual things.

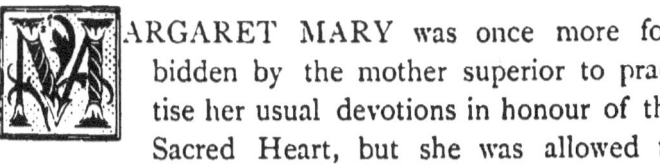ARGARET MARY was once more forbidden by the mother superior to practise her usual devotions in honour of the Sacred Heart, but she was allowed to resume them soon afterwards on account of the following miracle. A youthful sister fell ill, and before long was in a dying state. When Margaret Mary begged the Lord to restore her to health, He made known to her inwardly that her illness was owing to His wrath against the mother superior for having forbidden the devotion towards His Sacred Heart, and that she would not get well until permission was granted again to her to receive Communion on the first Friday of the month. Margaret Mary was afraid to tell this to Mother Greyfié, but she wrote as follows to a sister in whom she had great confidence : " This morning, when getting up, I seemed to hear distinctly these words : ' Say to your superior that she has offended Me much by forbidding you, in order to please creatures, the Communion which I ordered you to receive on the first Friday of every month, that by

offering Me to My eternal Father His divine justice might be satisfied for the faults which are committed against charity, since I have chosen you to be its victim. I have therefore determined to sacrifice to Myself the victim that now suffers.' See, my dear sister, what it is that torments and pursues me constantly; so that I cannot withdraw my thoughts from it because it continually urges me to make it known to our mother. To speak candidly, I am afraid to do it, for I think that it is merely a trick of the enemy who wishes to make me singular by this Communion; or that it is only a fancy and illusion; because it is not to a wretched hypocrite like me that our Lord would show such favour. I beg you, dear sister, to let me know what you think about it, in order to deliver me from this trouble. Do me this kindness without flattery, lest you withstand God; and I cannot tell what I suffer from beholding our sister in this state. Ask Him to make known the truth to you, and what He wills that you should say to me, and after that I will try to think no more about it. I beg you to burn this note, and to keep my secret." This sister advised Margaret Mary to make the matter known to the mother superior. She therefore made it known, and the mother superior gave her permission, but somewhat vaguely, to resume her devotions in honour of the Sacred Heart. Margaret Mary then prayed fervently for the recovery of the sister who was sick, and she at once became much better, but did not altogether recover her health. Margaret Mary con-

tinued to pray for her, but she nevertheless felt that
her prayer would not be heard until she had again
begun her devotions. She warned the mother superior that the Lord would not bestow perfect health
upon the sister unless she once more practised the
devotions which He had enjoined. She got the
fullest permission, and the sick sister became perfectly well. Margaret Mary therefore began again
to spend an hour at midnight every week prostrate
in prayer before the Blessed Sacrament, and to receive Communion on the first Friday of every month;
and Jesus Christ was faithful to His promise, and
opened wide His Sacred Heart to flood her soul with
graces and blessings.

Another miracle happened shortly afterwards in the
convent. The nuns of the Visitation Order led a
contemplative life, and had strict monastic enclosure,
but children who showed signs of a vocation to their
Order were allowed to dwell as little sisters amongst
them, and ladies who wished to go through the spiritual exercises spent some days in the convent. Women
and young girls sometimes assembled there on Sunday
in order to get religious instruction from the nuns, and
many visitors were wont to come and converse with
the Religious in the parlour. Margaret Mary had the
utmost dislike to spend her time speaking with those
who lived in the midst of the world. It happened
that a little sister who was only thirteen years of age
got a stroke of apoplexy, in the month of April, 1684,
and fell into a lethargic sleep. Margaret Mary, at the

bidding of her superior, prayed to Jesus Christ to
deign to restore the child to consciousness in order
that she might receive the last Sacraments; but He
said to her that the dying girl would not become conscious unless she herself made a vow to go to the
parlour whenever she was summoned there.   No
sooner had she made this vow than the little sister
regained consciousness, and, after devoutly receiving
the last Sacraments, she died a peaceful death shortly
afterwards.   Margaret Mary, although she hated the
world, never failed thenceforth to go to the convent
parlour whenever any body wished to speak to her.
Many from Paray and its neighbourhood came to see
her, and, whilst some spoke to her as to a Saint, others
treated her with scorn and contumely.   She bore
patiently with their rude behaviour, and kept her
soul in peace.   She was, indeed, a true anchoress,
for "true anchoresses," as an Anglo-Saxon writer
of the olden time says, "are birds of heaven that
fly aloft and sit upon the green boughs singing
merrily, that is, they meditate enraptured on the
blessedness of heaven that never fadeth, but is ever
green, and they sit on this green singing right merrily,
that is, in such meditation they rest in peace and have
gladness of heart as those who sing.   A bird, however,
sometimes alights down upon the earth in order to seek
his food for the need of the flesh; but while he sits
upon the ground he is never secure, and is often turning himself and always looking cautiously all around.
Even so the pious recluse, though she fly never so

high, must, at times, alight down to the earth; but then, as the bird doth, she must look well to herself and turn her eyes on every side, lest she be deceived and be caught in some of the devil's snares, or hurt in any way, while she sits so low."[1]   These worldly conversations, which were so distasteful to her because they took her away from the contemplation of God, were very profitable to her soul, and she learned by experience the truth of the teaching of Saint Francis of Sales. "Necessary employments, according to each one's vocation, do not lessen divine love but increase it, and, as it were, gild the work of devotion.   The nightingale loves her melody no less when she pauses than when she sings: the devout heart loves no less when she turns to exterior necessities than when she prays: her silence and her speech, her action and her contemplation, her employment and her rest, equally sing in her the hymn of her love."[2]

Margaret Mary still suffered from spiritual dryness, and from fears of being misled by the devil.   Mother Greyfié then wrote to her the following words of advice in order to comfort her in her sorrows: "May our Lord, who afflicts you according to His good pleasure, both in body and in mind, be also, by His grace and the mercy of His loving Heart, the strength and consolation of your whole being, both bodily and spiritually.   Such, my beloved sister and dear child, is the wish I make you, and is my reply to your note in which you describe your present state.   I see no-

---

[1] *Ancren Riwle.*   [2] *Love of God,* xii. 1.

thing in it which need make you afraid. Suffer or be glad peacefully according as God gives crosses or holy affections to your soul. I grant you, during the remainder of the time that I am in charge of this community, Holy Communion on the first Friday of each month, according to the intention of the Sacred Heart of Jesus Christ. I, moreover, grant it to you the last Saturday also of every month until I am deposed, in honour of the Blessed Virgin, that she may obtain from the Divine Heart of her Son a mother superior, who may be like Him and according to His will; and that she may obtain for me the grace of a true and deep humility, by means of which I may be able to please Him who resists the proud and gives His grace to the humble. I hope that I shall always get leave, when I will not be able to take it myself, to receive Communion on the Friday after the Octave of Corpus Christi as long as I live, as the late excellent Father de la Colombiere declared to be the desire of our Lord." Mother Greyfié ceased soon afterwards to be superior at Paray, and Mother Melin, who had lived there for thirty-three years, was chosen superior in her stead, in the month of May, 1684.

CHAPTER XI.

EV. MOTHER MELIN was "gentleness, wisdom, and piety itself," and she was looked upon as a living likeness of the sweet and humble Saint Francis of Sales. She had a great esteem and love for Margaret Mary, and immediately made her mother assistant. She was alarmed at getting this dignity and at being treated so well by the new superior, and she wrote to Mother Greyfié: "How can I feel so great a hunger for humiliations and sufferings, beset as I am with so many faults and miseries. Whenever I call to mind your goodness in bestowing this pleasant food some-times upon me, which is, indeed, disagreeable to nature, and how I am now deprived of this happiness, owing, doubtless, to the bad use I made of it, I feel over-whelmed with sorrow." Jesus Christ taught her, during her next retreat, to sacrifice her whole self to Him by love, worship, and conformity to the life which He leads in the Blessed Sacrament, and she resolved to be silent in remembrance of His V

silence there: to speak in honour of the Eternal
Word hidden there: when eating, to think of that
Divine Food: when reposing, to think of His
mysterious sleep within the Tabernacle: and to
bear her troubles and mortifications as an atonement for the insults which He there receives. She
also resolved to offer her prayers in union with the
prayer which the Sacred Heart ever offers up in the
Blessed Sacrament: at the end of every work to offer
it to the Sacred Heart in order that It might remedy
its defects, and to place each evening in that Adorable
Heart all that she had done during the day, in order
that It might purify and perfect whatever was faulty
and imperfect in her actions, and might make them
worthy to be placed in His Sacred Heart to be dis-
posed of according to His good pleasure.

Margaret Mary became mistress of novices six
months after her appointment as mother assistant.
Six young maidens, most of whom were of high birth
and wealthy, were then making their noviceship, and
Sister Anne-Alexis, who had been a professed Religious for four years, was with them by her own desire.
Margaret Mary watched with great love over this chosen
and holy flock, and won their love by her great gentleness and kindness towards them. She led them forward on the narrow path of religious perfection both
by word and by example; consoled them in their
sorrows; rejoiced with them in their joys; helped
them in their troubles; listened to them with patience
when they spoke to her; and nursed them like a

mother when they were ill. She reproved and
punished them, indeed, for their faults, and was
especially severe with them when they yielded to
sloth, frivolity, grumbling, vanity, and particular
friendships. She endeavoured, above all, to fill
their souls with the fire of the love of God, and
also sought to make them love their holy Rule.
Her sweet and loving words had a powerful effect
on these innocent souls. "Although," said one of
them afterwards, "we had learned all these ob-
servances from former mistresses, the venerable
sister explained them to us with a heavenly unction that seemed to flow from the Heart of Jesus,
and this made virtue easy for us;" and her outward
bearing and burning words of love to Jesus Christ
made such an impression upon them that they
likened her to the beloved disciple Saint John.

She often exclaimed, when she was in the midst of
these guileless maidens, "Oh, if you knew how sweet
it is to love God!" and she often said to them that
she would willingly suffer every torment in order to
save a single soul. She wished the novices to make
known to her all their spiritual difficulties, their
temptations, their failings, as well as their attractions
and good inspirations; and they had such confidence
in her goodness and her wisdom, that they freely and
frankly laid bare their whole soul to her, in order to
be guided safely by this holy mistress on the narrow
pathway of perfection. God gave her light to know
their spiritual wants, and to choose suitable remedies

for their souls. She gave her answers to their difficulties mostly in writing, and these writings, which
still exist, show forth clearly both her wisdom and her
holiness. She was ever praying for her novices, and
she laid their wants, their failings, their temptations,
and their troubles before Jesus Christ, begging Him
to help them and to guide them. She offered up all
her penances and her good works for their spiritual
welfare, and she never reproved them or gave them
advice until she had first prayed to the Sacred Heart
for light and grace.

The novices grew in holiness through the influence
of her example and of her teaching, and never became
weary of well-doing, but ever went forward gladly from
virtue to virtue. They made war on their passions,
overcame their evil inclinations, and subdued their
self-love and self-will; they weeded the garden of
their soul, in order that the flowers of virtue might
bloom in them; they dug deep foundations, in order
to build a lofty building of perfection; and they
changed the thorns of their faults and failings into
roses by humble accusation and penance. They
crucified their flesh, with its vices and concupiscences,
and having healed the maladies of their souls by the
bitter medicine of inward and outward mortification,
they, with ease and gladness, practised virtue, and
flew swiftly by good works towards union with God.
They all soon reached a high degree of perfection,
and the love of God grew apace in their souls. The
thought of their Beloved watching like an angel by

their bedside whilst they slept gladdened them when they awoke, helped them to pray, soothed their sorrows, made their labours light, and gave them strength always to do His holy will. They thus led the life of angels upon earth, ever holding a sword in their hands to make war on the foes of their salvation, whilst building the edifice of religious perfection. They gave great delight to the Sacred Heart of Jesus Christ, for "as the freshness of the spring morning is more agreeable than any other portion of the day, so also are the virtues acquired in youth more pleasing in the sight of God ".[1]

Margaret Mary often spoke to the novices on the love of the Sacred Heart, but never mentioned her visions and revelations to them. She taught them to show great love for Jesus Christ, who had died on the cross and still lived on earth in the Blessed Sacrament out of love for them ; to acknowledge this love by affectionate and grateful love, and by outward practices of devotion ; and to make reparation to His loving Heart for all the ungratefulness and insults which He received during His life, and which He still received daily in the Blessed Sacrament. A novice found in a book, which Margaret Mary had lent to her, a paper in her handwriting, which contained these words : "Our Lord made known to me this evening whilst I was at prayer that He wished to be known, loved, and honoured by men, and that He would therefore bestow many graces upon them,

---

[1] Saint John of the Cross.

whenever they should consecrate themselves to the devotion and love of His Sacred Heart". She showed this writing to the other novices, and they then knew that the burning words of their mistress about the Sacred Heart were the outcome of revelations granted to her by Jesus Christ. The spiritual retreat of Father de la Colombiere, which had lately been printed, was shortly afterwards read during mealtime in the refectory, and the reader was the novice who had found the writing of Margaret Mary. When, during the reading, she came to the passage where the holy Jesuit spoke of the devotion to the Sacred Heart, she glanced at the novice mistress, who was seated in front of her; but Margaret Mary hung down her head, and became absorbed in prayer. She then read from the book the following words: "I have learned that God wishes me to serve Him by obtaining the fulfilment of His wishes with regard to the devotion which He made known to a person to whom He speaks very familiarly, and for whose sake He has used my weakness. I have already taught it to many in England; and I have written about this devotion to France, and have begged one of my friends there to spread it: it will do much good. God having communicated Himself then to the person, who, as we have reason to think, is according to His Heart, by the great graces which He has granted her, she spoke to me about it, and I commanded her to put what she said in writing. I myself desired to write it in my book of retreats, because God wishes to make

use of my feeble efforts in the fulfilment of this
design." The account of the vision of the Sacred
Heart then followed. The nuns and novices were
wonderstruck at what they heard, and they understood that it was Margaret Mary who had made these
predictions. The novice who had read said to her
when the meal was over, "My dear mother, there was
much about you in to-day's reading"; and the humble
novice mistress, hanging down her head, said, "I have
good reason to love my lowliness". The novices
henceforth looked upon her as a saint, and carefully
kept bits of her Religious dress and even some of her
hair as relics. She thenceforward spoke to them
oftener and more openly about the devotion to the
Sacred Heart, and she placed a small picture of the
Sacred Heart, made with ink, upon the altar of the
novitiate, on the Friday after the Octave of Corpus
Christi, in the year 1685.

The festival of Saint Margaret, July 20, was the
feast day of the mistress of novices, and the novices
who loved and revered made great preparations to
keep it worthily. But she asked them one day
whether they wished to make her happy thereby, and
when they answered that they very much wished it,
she begged them for the love which they bore to her
to give to the Sacred Heart of Jesus Christ all the
honour which they had intended to give to her. "I
found no means of making known the devotion to the
Sacred Heart, which was all that I wished for. The
following was the first opportunity which His goodness

gave to me. The feast of Saint Margaret, my patron
saint, happening to come on a Friday, I begged our
novice sisters, of whom I had care at the time, to pay
to the Sacred Heart of our Lord whatever little signs
of respect they intended on that day to pay to me.
They gladly agreed to do it. They accordingly got
ready a little altar, and put upon it a small picture of
the Sacred Heart sketched with a pen. We endeavoured to show to it every sign of honour with
which the Divine Heart inspired us. This drew upon
me and upon them also many humiliations, contradictions, and mortifications." [1] The novices without the
knowledge of Margaret Mary had made an altar in a
recess beneath a flight of stairs, and had decorated
it with roses, and they had put a small paper picture
of the Sacred Heart in the midst. They spent nearly
the whole of the night before the festival, with the
leave of the mother superior, fitting up the altar and
painting the walls and the ceiling of the room with
flowers, stars, and hearts. They led Margaret Mary
there the following morning after Prime. As soon as
she had come to the novitiate, and when she beheld
what they had done she was overjoyed, thanked them
warmly, and spoke to them like a seraph. She
prostrated herself before the picture and consecrated
herself to the Sacred Heart, and each of the novices
did likewise. Margaret Mary in the afternoon once
more gathered together her little flock around the
altar; and after having broken forth into burning

[1] *Memoir.*

words of love towards the Sacred Heart of Jesus
Christ, she said that she would be glad if the whole
community came to give honour to it.   A novice
immediately went to beg the nuns to come and show
honour to the Sacred Heart, but they all with the
exception of two or three refused the invitation, saying
that it was not becoming that novices should establish
new devotions, and that it was forbidden by the Rule.
Sister Mary Magdalen des Escures, who was called
by her fellow-Religious   "The holy mother Mary
Magdalen" and "The Living Rule," said sharply to
her: "Go tell your mistress that good devotion
consists in the practice of our Rules and Constitutions,
and that is what she ought to teach you and which
you should practise".

The novice, when she had returned to the novitiate,
merely said that the sisters could not come, but
Margaret Mary answered : "Say rather that they are
unwilling: the Sacred Heart, however, will make
them come ; they are now opposed to it ; but the day
shall come when they will be the most eager of all ".
The novice mistress and the novices spent the whole
day in a holy joy, and towards evening Margaret
Mary spoke the following words to them : "No ! my
dear sisters you could not have given a more heartfelt pleasure to me, than by thus paying honour to the
Divine Heart of Jesus Christ, and by consecrating
yourselves entirely to Him.   How happy you are, that
He has been pleased to make use of you to begin the
practice of this devotion.   Let us continue to pray

that He may reign in all hearts. Oh, how glad I am
that this Heart of my Divine Master will be known,
loved, and honoured. Yes, my dear sisters, it is the
greatest comfort which I can receive in this life to see
Him reign everywhere. Let us then love, but without
reserve, and without making any exception; let us
give everything and sacrifice everything to gain this
happiness, and we shall have everything in possessing
the Heart of God."

The nuns, meanwhile, did not cease to grumble at
this innovation, and they strongly urged the mother
superior to hinder the spreading of it. She, however,
well knew the great holiness of Margaret Mary, and held
her in the highest esteem, but for the sake of peace
she forbade her to practise the devotion to the Sacred
Heart in future outside of the novitiate. The sisters,
led away by a false zeal, were never weary of upbraiding
and finding fault with her, and they even threatened to
denounce her to the superiors of the Order. The
younger sisters sometimes thoughtlessly teased her
with merry jests and stinging witticisms, but whilst
feeling these railleries most keenly—for "the stroke of
a whip makes a blue mark, but the stroke of the
tongue will break the bones"[1]—she bore them
meekly, knowing well that suffering is the food of the
love of God.

[1] Ecclesiasticus xxviii.

CHAPTER XII.

ARGARET MARY wrote about a month
after her feast day to her former superior,
Mother de Saumaise, who was then
superior of the Visitation convent at
Dijon, and made known to her what had happened
amongst the novices, and that a youth from Paris,
who was a relative of one of them, having learnt at
Paray about the devotion to the Sacred Heart, had
undertaken most eagerly to have a picture of the
Sacred Heart painted, provided they gave him a
design for it. She begged Mother de Saumaise to
help her, and promised many blessings to her on the
part of Jesus Christ if she would endeavour to spread
the devotion to His Sacred Heart. "Our Lord has
made known to me that all who are devout to the
Sacred Heart should not be lost, and that as He is
the fountain of all blessings, He would bestow them
plentifully wherever a picture of this amiable Heart
should be placed to be loved and venerated ; that
He would, through it, bring back harmony in dis-

united families; that He would protect those who were in want, and that He would give a special grace of salvation and sanctity to whoever would be foremost in having this picture made ". She again wrote to her the following words : " I would be very glad to know whether you are willing to do something which has been chosen and reserved for you by the Sacred Heart of our good Master ; I mean that as you were the first to whom He was pleased that I should make known the burning desire which He has to be known, loved, and worshipped by creatures, He wishes you to have an engraven plate made of this Sacred Heart, in order that all those who desire to show Him some honour might have pictures in their houses and smaller ones to bear about upon themselves. It seems to me that it would be a great happiness for you to obtain this honour for Him, for which you shall get a greater reward than for anything else which you have done during your lifetime."

Margaret Mary likewise wrote to Mother Greyfié, who was then superior in the convent at Semur : " If you knew, my good Mother, how much I feel myself urged to love the Sacred Heart of our Lord Jesus Christ ! It seems to me that it is for that alone I have got life. He has favoured me with a visit, which has been very useful to me on account of the good impressions which it has left in my heart. He has assured me again that the pleasure which He takes in being loved, known, and honoured by His creatures is so great that, if I am not deceived, He has promised to me that those who are devout to Him shall never be lost, and that as He is the fountain of all blessings, he will bestow them abundantly wherever the picture of His Sacred Heart shall be placed and venerated." Mother Greyfié had finished reading the *Retreat of Father de la Colombiere* when she got this letter, and although she had formerly been somewhat distrustful of the visions and revelations of Margaret Mary she now believed in them, and at once got an oil painting of the Sacred Heart made, and placed it over the altar in an oratory in the monastery, and then, kneeling before it, together with the whole community, they consecrated themselves publicly and solemnly to the Sacred Heart of Jesus Christ. She sent a copy of this painting, as well as twelve sketches in ink of it, to Margaret Mary and her novices.

Margaret Mary was overjoyed when she received these pictures, and at once made presents of some of them to those who were most devout to the Sacred Heart. She gave one of them to the Jesuit Fathers at Paray, and sent another to Mother de Saumaise at Dijon. She wrote, in answer to the letter of Mother Greyfié : " I thought, my dear Mother, that you would tell me to give up all idea of introducing this devotion of the Sacred Heart, and to think of it as merely a foolish effect of my imagination, and I therefore kept my mind in a state of submission, because I give slight heed to anything that comes from myself ; but when I beheld the picture of that one object of our love sent by you, I seemed to begin a new life. I was hitherto steeped in a sea of sorrow and suffering, and God has changed it into such great peace and submission to all the arrangements of His heavenly providence in my regard, that I feel as if nothing could give me any trouble. My only wish is to procure glory for this Sacred Heart, and how happy would I be if I could gain this before I die. You can help me much, my dear Mother, by reassuring my poor and feeble courage, which takes fright at everything. But I wander from my subject. It seemed to me then that some names were written on that Sacred Heart because of their wish to give it honour, and therefore He will never allow them to be blotted out; but He did not inform me that these friends should get no crosses, for He wills that their chief happiness should consist in tasting the bitterness of sorrow. Can it be that we would not wish to love Him with our whole strength in spite of these contradictions. They do not fail us, as you know; but I am resolved, with the help of this Adorable Heart, either to die or to overcome these hindrances. I cannot tell you what comfort you have given to me by sending this beautiful picture, as well as by your willingness to help us by joining, together with your community, in our devotion. This news gave me ten thousand times more joy than if you had given to me all the wealth of the world."

Many of the nuns at Paray became devout to the

Sacred Heart as soon as they had heard what Mother Greyfié had done, for they knew well her great wisdom, her love of the Rule, and her distrust of extraordinary spiritual favours. A great storm, however, burst at the same time upon Margaret Mary through a daughter of the Count de Chamron, who was then a novice under her care at the convent. This young lady was there through fear of her father, and against her own will, but she behaved as a fervent novice, and always declared that she wished to become a nun. Margaret Mary, however, was enlightened by God with a knowledge of the truth, and she induced her to go away. The father of the young lady was very much offended and threatened the nuns, and, above all, the holy mistress of the novices. His relatives were also full of wrath against her, and everywhere declared her to be a visionary, a hypocrite, and an impostor. The Cardinal of Bouillon, who was a friend of the family, spoke very bitterly about her, and she ran a great risk of being thrown into prison. A Religious of high birth and great holiness, who was also a friend of the family, took the part of the young lady and became a great enemy of Margaret Mary. She bore all this tribulation patiently for the love of the Sacred Heart of Jesus Christ ; and she said to the novices : " It is He Himself who has allowed us to meet with this cross in order to prepare us for His feast ". Many of the nuns, frightened by the wrath of these powerful persons, and fearing that no more novices would enter the convent, often spoke angrily and harshly to her, and never grew weary of telling her that she was misled by the devil, and that she was a scandal to the community. She then began, herself, to be afraid that she was deceived by the devil, and she wrote the following letter to Mother de Saumaise : " I am afflicted in many ways, but the severest trial is having to look on myself as the sport of the devil. I see nothing in myself but what deserves punishment, as I have been not only so unhappy as to deceive myself, but also to deceive others by my hypocrisy—though, as it appears to me, without intending it. I can no longer doubt it after the opinion of this great servant of God. I have reason to thank God a thousand times for having sent him to me to un-deceive those who had been kind enough to have some esteem for me. What special thanks I owe him throughout my whole life on account of having done me this great service! I assure you that nothing gives me more comfort than to know, that creatures being undeceived, I shall be able to satisfy the justice of God, and be for ever despised. This thought soothes me and softens all that I suffer."

Margaret Mary distrusted herself and looked upon herself as worthless and without virtue ; but she was saved from deception by her childlike trust in her confessor, Father Rolin, a very holy Jesuit father who was then living at Paray. She laid everything before him in writing, and he wrote her the following answer to her doubts : " I have read, my dear sister

in our Lord, your two letters, and I thank God for all
the mercies which He shows to you. I will answer
each with all the sincerity that God requires of me.
The spirit that guides you is not a spirit of darkness :
its guidance is good, for it is always submissive to
obedience, and leaves you at peace when your superior
has spoken. In the next place you shall see my
thoughts as before God. They are not devils who
are enraged against you. The spirit of darkness is
not the cause of the persecutions you experience, it is
divine love which acts, and, to my great consolation,
uses souls that are dear to Him to make you suffer.
The martyrs had not this consolation in their torments;
their tyrants committed great crimes in afflicting them,
but the holy souls who procure crosses for you please
God in the little martyrdom which they make you
suffer. This thought ought to give you much comfort. I am willing that you should attribute to your
faults whatever happens, though all this may be an
effect of the goodness of God rather than of His
justice. All the names which they call you, which
are so humbling, ought to make nothing come forth
from your mouth save thanksgivings to our Lord, and
prayers for those who utter them. Do not repent of
anything which you have spoken. A cause which
brings forth such excellent crosses cannot be bad.
Let them complain as much as they like, and fear
nothing on my account. When all they can say
against you is repeated to the whole world, it will be
the greatest favour which our Lord can bestow on you.

Let them tell whomsoever they will, you ought to rejoice at it. Expulsion, imprisonment, all comes from the love of Jesus Christ for you. I ask from you a perfect self-abandonment and a heart ready to do everything and to suffer everything. I repeat what I have said, you are not the sport of Satan, but of the divine love, for it is the language of Scripture that sacred love has its rigours whether because it is the offspring of Mount Calvary, or because it partakes of the divine justice which wishes to satisfy itself in afflicting us." This letter of her holy director gave great peace to her soul, and great comfort in her troubles. Father Rolin had been greatly prejudiced against Margaret Mary when he came to Paray the year before, but he quickly learned from what he himself saw and heard that she was a saint, and that she was favoured in a very special way by the Lord. He helped her thenceforth in all her difficulties and consoled her in all her sorrows.

The reverend mother superior also took her part always, and told her at the beginning of the year 1686 that she had the hope that the community would build a chapel which should have in it a beautiful painting of the Sacred Heart.

CHAPTER XIII.

ARGARET MARY had once foretold that the sisters who were the most opposed to the devotion of the Sacred Heart would be amongst the first to establish it, but they scoffed at this prediction. God, however, suddenly changed their hearts. Sister Mary Magdalen des Escures loved and esteemed Margaret Mary, but she was a great foe to the new devotion, for she thought that it was contrary to the simplicity and to the Rules of the Visitation Order. She was urged by an irresistible impulse from the Holy Ghost, one day during the Octave of Corpus Christi, in the year 1686, to acknowledge publicly her mistake and to make atonement for her unbelief. She struggled strongly against this inspiration, but grace triumphed over her repugnance and fears, and she resolved to make a solemn reparation to the Sacred Heart of Jesus Christ. She spoke to the mother superior about it, and with her permisssion she at once began to make preparations for this public act of reparation.

10

She went, on Thursday evening, to the novitiate, and begged Margaret Mary to lend her the picture of the Sacred Heart, which had been sent to her by Mother Greyfié. Margaret Mary knew by an inspiration the reason of her request, and willingly gave the picture to her, and she, together with the novices, prayed much for the good success of the undertaking. Sister Mary Magdalen, very early the next morning, erected a small altar in front of the grating in the nuns' choir, and put the picture of the Sacred Heart upon it, in the midst of flowers and of lighted candles. She also wrote an invitation to the nuns to consecrate themselves to the Sacred Heart, signed it with her name, and placed it over the picture.

When the nuns came that morning into the choir and saw the altar and the picture, moved by a sudden impulse of the Holy Ghost, they knelt before it and consecrated their hearts to the Sacred Heart of Jesus Christ. They spent almost the whole of that day, the first Friday after the Octave of Corpus Christi, venerating the picture of the Sacred Heart, which was enthroned amidst lights and flowers upon the little altar in their choir, and they resolved to build a chapel in honour of the Sacred Heart in the convent garden. The sisters who had incomes from their relatives spent their money on it; the little sisters saved their pocket-money for the same purpose, and the lay sisters worked harder, in order to earn money for the furtherance of that holy object.

The novices meanwhile placed their picture of the

Sacred Heart in a conspicuous part of the house, where all might show honour to it, and they carefully decorated it every day with fresh and fragrant flowers gathered in the garden. Margaret Mary was filled to overflowing with consolation, and she joyfully exclaimed, " I now have nothing more to desire, since the Heart of my Saviour is beginning to be known and to reign in the hearts of men ". She then sang a *Te Deum*, together with the happy novices, in thanksgiving to God for the outburst of devotion towards the Sacred Heart of Jesus Christ ; and she also wrote a letter of thanks to Sister Mary Magdalen. This sister thenceforth took charge of the oratory which had been erected by the nuns in honour of the Sacred Heart.

Margaret Mary knew, from the teaching of Jesus Christ, how pleasing it was to Him that men should love and worship Him, and that they should show honour to His Sacred Heart, which is the symbol of His love for them; and she also knew that this devotion was a most efficacious means of obtaining graces and salvation. She therefore wrote as follows : " I do not know if there is any devotion in the spiritual life more suitable to lift up the soul speedily to higher holiness and to make it taste the true sweetness which is to be found in the service of God. Yes, I say with certainty, that if it were known how pleasing this devotion is to Jesus Christ, there is not a Christian, howsoever weak may be his love for this amiable Saviour, who would not at once practise it. Endeavour to get all religious persons to take it up, for they shall obtain so much help from it that nothing shall be needful to restore the first fervour and the utmost regularity to the most ill-regulated communities, and to lead those who already live in observant convents to high perfection. My Divine Saviour has shown me that those who work for the salvation of souls shall have the skill to move the hardest hearts, and shall labour with wonderful success if they are themselves full of a tender devotion to His Divine Heart. As for persons living in the world, they shall by its means get all the help which is needful to them for their state of life, namely, peace in their families, assistance in their works, and the blessing of Heaven upon all their undertakings. It is, indeed in this adorable Heart that they will find a place of refuge during life, and especially at the hour of death. Oh, how sweet it is to die after having had a constant devotion to the Sacred Heart of Him who is to judge us! In a word, there certainly is no one in the world who will not obtain every sort of help from Heaven if he has a grateful love for Jesus Christ, such as that which is shown towards Him by the devotion to His Sacred Heart."

The devotion to the Sacred Heart speedily spread throughout the south of France, and the Religious of Paray, Semur, and Dijon were unwearied in their efforts to make that beautiful devotion grow and flourish amongst the faithful by means of pictures and books. A book in praise of the devotion, which was written by a Visitation nun at Dijon, was published, with the permission of the Bishop of Langres, at the end of the year 1686; and another book, containing a Litany of the Sacred Heart, together with some prayers composed by Margaret Mary, was also published about the same time. An Office of the Sacred Heart also was written and published by a Jesuit father. These books caused a widespread outburst of devotion throughout France to the Sacred Heart of Jesus Christ. The devotion, however, met with great opposition, as the most holy Redeemer had met with opposition when He dwelt on earth. France was then infected with a spirit of lawlessness, of pride, of a servile fear and half-hearted love of God, and the wicked disciples of Jansenism opposed with might and main a devotion which had been revealed by God in order to re-enkindle the fire of a tender love to Jesus Christ within the hearts of men. Margaret Mary was very sorrowful at this opposition of evil-minded men, but she prayed and prophesied that the devotion to the Sacred Heart would triumph despite their wiles. She wrote the following letter about it to her former mother superior, Mother de Saumaise, who had become a faithful servant of the Sacred Heart and a warm advocate of the newly-revealed devotion:

" I clearly perceive, my dear Mother, that all those little oppositions to our amiable devotion astonish you, and, if I am not mistaken, grieve you deeply. But why should it be so, since it seems you have been already warned that Satan would rise up against it; angry as he is to see that by this salutary means

he will lose many souls, which he believed to be in
his own keeping, and that some have been already
taken from him, and many more will be drawn away
by the Almighty power of Him, who in His own good
time will turn all these oppositions and contradictions
to His greater glory and the confusion of the enemy
of our souls.   He will even make use of this opposition as a solid foundation on which to establish this
holy devotion, for which purpose He makes us resolve
generously to bear all the difficulties in the way, and
the efforts of Satan against it.   It is even said that the
clergy have orders not to allow any new devotions to
be practised in their parishes, and that this one to the
Divine Heart is already forbidden in some places.
They say, moreover, that all the booksellers are to
receive orders not to print anything on this subject,
and several other things of the same kind are reported;
but all this does not in the least astonish me.   I have
such great confidence that the Lord will finish what
He has begun, that it seems to me I should have no
fears if much more were said and done against it; but
if it is not His good pleasure that we should succeed
more rapidly, we must be resigned to His holy will,
as it is that alone which we seek to do, and should
therefore leave everything to Him.   I assure you,
dear Mother, that although there is nothing in the
world that I so eagerly desire, or which is so dear to
my heart, and the bad success of which would be
more deeply felt by me, than this devotion, yet I am
so resigned to whatever it should please our Lord to

arrange, that I shall be equally satisfied with whatever
may happen, because I only desire the will of my God
in all things.   I often say to Him : ' Lord, it is Thy
affair : I know that if Thou willest, it will infallibly
succeed, notwithstanding all the obstacles that may
be raised against it ; but if Thou dost not will it, in
vain shall we labour : Thou wilt overturn all our
designs ; but if this devotion is for Thy glory, dispose
all things so that it may succeed to Thy honour ; and
for that purpose make Thyself Master of their hearts '.
I have heard no news for some time of that good
Religious of Lyons who labours for the glory of this
holy Heart.   He wrote to me three times without
receiving any answer from me.   A short time ago I
wrote to him by obedience, but I do not know
whether he has received my letter.   I confess, dear
Mother, that you are right in not approving my
manner of acting with regard to letter-writing and the
parlour ; but if you knew my reasons for doing this I
think that you would advise me to do so always.   God
be blessed for all things.   Let us pray continually and
act, without growing weary, for the interests of the
amiable Heart of Jesus.

" Believe me that I am always yours in His love."

A Jesuit father came from Lyons to Paray, and he
undertook at her suggestion to have a copperplate
engraving made. She gave him a design for it, but, as
he was ever going about the country busy giving missions to the people, he probably forgot all about his
promise ; at least he failed to get the engraving made;

and Margaret Mary, with considerable trouble, got back her drawing from him. She sent it forthwith to Mother de Saumaise, and begged her to get a better drawing of the Sacred Heart made at Dijon, and then to have it engraved. Sister Johanna Joly, who was an inmate of the Visitation convent in that town, made a beautiful drawing of the Sacred Heart, according to the design sent by Margaret Mary, and sent it to Paray. It was shortly afterwards engraved at Paris, and numerous copies were taken from it. Margaret Mary wrote the following letter to thank her for her kindness, and for her devotion to the Sacred Heart.

"I confess to you, my dear Sister, that I feel my heart capable of no other joy or satisfaction than that which I receive from the increase of the glory of this amiable Heart: it is at times so great that it would be very difficult for me to explain my feelings. I rejoice at what you tell me, and especially at the news that a good Capuchin father is so much interested in this devotion; for Jesus takes pleasure in the services of the humble of heart, and bestows great blessings upon their labours. I trust that all you point out regarding the devotion to this Divine Heart will be done in good time; but we must wait with patience, for grace acts gently and sweetly, though strongly and efficaciously; He wills, however, that we should be faithful and prompt in following His lights and movements. Oh, how happy we are, my dear Sister, and how much we are indebted to this Divine Heart, for condescending to make use of us for the accomplishment of this grand design ! He will bestow great treasures on all those who are employed in it, and who carefully use all the helps He gives them for that purpose. You cannot think how much this devotion has increased, spreading graces and blessings everywhere. There are some priests in large towns who establish it in their parishes as soon as they become acquainted with its merits; and even some of great learning and piety, after having been strongly opposed to it, now preach it to the people, and say that there is no devotion more salutary or holy. You will see a very striking instance of this in the letter I send to Sister de Saumaise, together with a newly-printed book which has been given to me. It is a pleasure to me to send it to her, and I would also send one to you if I had a second, but I hope she will share it with you. You will see good reason to bless the Lord, and I think that he who composed it will not stop there. God grant that it may be so. I would willingly give my life in thanksgiving for all these happy beginnings: in this progress is all my joy and consolation. I seem to be insensible to everything else. Our Lord presses me so ardently to love Him, and cause Him to be loved, that were it necessary to suffer for that object all labours, pains, and sorrows, they would all be turned into joys, and there is no suffering which I would not gladly endure. I would even accept, if I may say so, the pains of hell to make Him reign ; since He appears to have so great a desire to bestow the treasures of His sanctifying and salutary graces upon souls, so great a number of which are lost to Him; but His goodness, in spite of the malice of Satan, will draw many from the way of perdition. Be sure, then, my dear Sister, to consider it a great happiness to be employed in this holy work. Do not fear to forget yourself for this object; the forgetfulness of self and every human interest is the very disposition He requires from those whom He so employs. He takes care at the same time not to forget you, for His love looks upon you with delight, and is occupied in purifying and sanctifying you, that you may be perfectly united to Himself, whilst you are employed in glorifying Him. He is pleased at your endeavours because He loves you; but if you could understand in what manner He loves you, you would place no limits to your exertions, that you might offer Him some little return. Complain no more of my silence, since it proceeds neither from forgetfulness nor indifference, but from the desire I have always to live poor and unknown to creatures; I could wish them only to remember this miserable sinner in order to despise and humble her; as well to give me what is justly my due so as to annihilate me still more in my love of abjection. I have reason to love it in everything, but especially when I consider that that amiable Heart has not been able to find one more poor, more vile, more weak and unworthy than myself for that work which is to procure Him so much glory, and for which I hope He will take care to furnish me with all necessary assistance. When Satan, in the beginning, raised oppositions and contradictions greater than I can tell you, His goodness always supported my courage, and animated me by those loving words which ever gave me confidence and assurance: 'What dost thou fear? I shall reign in spite of Satan and all those who oppose Me.' But, alas! my dear Sister, how much reason I have to fear that by my ingratitude and unfaithfulness I have been an obstacle to the establishment of His kingdom. This makes me feel that I had rather a thousand times He should withdraw me from the face of the earth without regarding my interests, than that I should be the slightest hindrance to His designs. But I am convinced that He wishes to establish His empire by gentleness and sweetness alone, and not by the rigour of His justice; for this reason, not wishing to lose me, He unites me in spiritual blessings with His most faithful friends, of whom your confessor is one, that by their love and fidelity they may repair the negligences committed by me in His holy service. I am persuaded that if these holy souls knew how wicked I am, they would never consent to this union, lest I should draw down upon them the indignation of this Sacred Heart, without which life would be an insupportable torment to me. We must then love Him with all our strength, whatever it may cost us. Should we not be happy if He judged us worthy to suffer for His love, in the flames of which I desire your heart may be always burning, until, being consumed and transferred into Him, it becomes one with Him? He alone knows how dear

He has made your heart to mine, which never forgets
you in His holy presence, any more than it does those
holy enterprises you have undertaken for His glory.
This is my principal intention in all my prayers, but
it seems to me that your love for this Divine Heart
ought to interest you a little in beseeching Him to
consume me with its most lively ardours that I may
learn to love Him; for, alas! I am ashamed to say
that I love Him, since I suffer nothing, or, at least, so
little, that it is a cruel martyrdom to me to do so, for
to wish to love God without suffering is only an
illusion; and yet I cannot understand how it can be
called suffering, when we truly love the Sacred Heart
of our Lord Jesus Christ, since He changes the
bitterness into sweetness, and causes delight in the
midst of pain and humiliation. But, dear Mother, if
the simple desire of ardently loving the Sacred Heart
can produce this effect, what effects will not be produced in those hearts that love it truly, and whose
greatest suffering is not to suffer enough, or rather not
to love enough? In truth, I believe that everything
is changed into love; and a soul which is once consumed with this sacred fire, has no other exercise or
employment than to love in suffering. Let us then
love our Sovereign Master; but let us love Him upon
the cross, for it is His delight to find in a heart, love,
suffering, and silence. You have found the secret of
making me break this silence, by speaking to me of
this amiable Heart of our Divine Saviour, on which
subject I cannot keep within bounds; but, alas! it

is only in words and not in deed. I hope the length
of this letter will prevent your complaining of my
silence for the future, and that you will permit me to
maintain it in the Heart of our amiable Jesus, where
I am entirely yours in sacred love."

CHAPTER XIV.

ARGARET MARY made a vow on the eve of the Feast of All Saints, by which she bound herself to unite, consecrate, and sacrifice her whole being more directly, absolutely, and perfectly to the Sacred Heart; and she was shortly afterwards rewarded for this offering of herself by a great spiritual favour, for after having received Holy Communion on the Feast of the beloved disciple Saint John, she beheld the Sacred Heart, and, deep down in her soul, heard loving words of promise and of complaint. Jesus Christ then made known to her His desire that His Sacred Heart should be honoured by men, and He promised many blessings to those who should honour It. " He showed me that His great desire of being perfectly loved by men had made Him resolve to show them His heart, and give in these latter days this last·effort of His love, offering to them an object and a means so suitable to make them love Him, and to love Him solidly : that in doing this, He opened to them all the treasures of love, grace, mercy, holiness, and salvation, which this Heart contains; in order that all those who wished to give Him and to get for Him all the love and honour in their power might be enriched with the abundance of treasures of which this Divine Heart is the fruitful and never failing fountain. He again assured me that He took a special pleasure in beholding the inward feelings of His Heart and of His love honoured under the figure of this Heart of flesh, such as had been shown to me, and that He wished it to be shown publicly, in order to move the hard hearts of men. He, at the same time, promised to me that He would pour out abundantly the treasures of grace with which His Heart is filled into the hearts of those who should honour Him, and that He would bestow every sort of blessing wherever this image should be exposed." [1]

Margaret Mary endeavoured to enkindle in the souls of the novices a burning love for Jesus Christ, together with a tender devotion to His Sacred Heart. She, however, urged strongly upon them the duty of loving Him even when they were afflicted and suffering from desolation of spirit, and she often said: " What a weakness to love Jesus Christ only when He caresses us, and to grow cold as soon as He reproves us ! Those who love Him in this way love themselves too much to love Jesus Christ with their whole heart." She taught them to show their love towards Him by always doing His holy will, and by

[1] *Memoir.*

bearing their sufferings patiently. She also taught them to practise blind obedience to their superiors and to their Rule, and she said to them : "The soul of this obedience consists in having no self-will, in having no desire which is not submissive, and in being ever willing to yield opinions, lights, and inclinations to the inclinations, opinions, and lights of our superiors ". She entreated them to take the Sacred Heart of Jesus as their model, and to be humble, to distrust their own judgment, to look on themselves as the least of all, and to be glad to be despised. She taught them the necessity of detachment even from the most trifling things, and that the Heart of Jesus Christ was the only treasure of a Religious.

She strove to make them hunger and thirst for Holy Communion, and she chided those who feared to go to the Holy Table, saying to them: "What would you say of a child who was afraid to go to his father and mother, and hid from their sight?" She, however, begged them never to go to Communion without making some sacrifice to Jesus Christ, either by an act of mortification, or by overcoming some evil inclination. She also often spoke to them of the wonderful worth of prayer, and she said : " A daughter of Mary who does not love prayer is a soldier without weapons, a fortress without walls, a ship without food, a lamp without oil " ; but she, nevertheless, taught them that they could not practise mental prayer aright unless they were mortified. She was sometimes in-

spired with a supernatural knowledge of the temptations and failings of the novices. A young and
somewhat giddy novice once felt a great dislike for
her novice mistress, because she was so serious, and
she hid the temptation through shame, but Margaret
Mary, one day, having spoken kindly and gently to
her about Religious perfection, mentioned the temptation to her, and the novice acknowledged it, and
thenceforth had a great love and esteem for her holy
mistress. She sometimes warned the novices of
afflictions that would befal them, and often foretold
events, and everything that she thus foretold sooner
or later happened.

Margaret Mary ceased to be novice mistress at the
beginning of the year 1687, and became instead
sister infirmarian, and some time afterwards mistress
of the children. Fifteen children were then living
in the convent as little sisters, but, as Margaret Mary
foretold, only two of them persevered and became
Visitation nuns. One day, one of these children
planted a fruit tree in the convent garden, and, whilst
planting it, said, laughingly, to her little companions—
" When I become a nun I shall eat the fruit on it " ;
but Margaret Mary overheard her, and said gravely to
her, " It is not worth your while to plant that tree,
for you shall not be a nun in this house," and the
girl, as her holy mistress had foretold, left the convent of the Visitation shortly afterwards, and became
an Ursuline nun at Paray. She was ever teaching
these guileless children to love Jesus Christ, and to

be very devout to His Sacred Heart. They, in after years, helped very much to make known that holy devotion. Rev. Mother Melin was chosen mother superior anew in the month of May, of the year 1687, and Margaret Mary again became mother assistant. She was now esteemed and loved by all her Sisters in Religion, and they eagerly followed her by being devout to the Sacred Heart of Jesus Christ.

The devotion to the Sacred Heart triumphed, in spite of all opposition, and every day brought good tidings of its onward progress. As the seafarer who, having drifted amidst midnight gloom upon the waves which burst far away upon the rocky shore, at length beholds the beams of the rising sun, and sees his ship sailing swiftly through the smooth water towards the golden cliffs at the entrance of the harbour, is filled with hope and gladness, so the heart of Margaret Mary overflowed with joy when she learned that the devotion which she loved so well had become wide-spread, and that the Sacred Heart of her beloved Lord had begun at length to be known and loved by men. Her sisters in Religion were busy building in the convent garden at Paray a small chapel in honour of the Sacred Heart of Jesus Christ, and her brother, James, who was parish priest at Bois Sainte Marie, was also helping to glorify It, on account of having been miraculously cured through means of his devotion to the Sacred Heart. He had fallen ill at the beginning of the year 1687, and having got a stroke of apoplexy, had become unconscious. His brother,

Chrysostom, at once sent a messenger in haste to Margaret Mary, begging her to pray for the recovery of their brother. She prayed very fervently for him, and then sent a paper, on which a prayer to the Sacred Heart was written to Chrysostom, bidding him dip it in water, and give the water to the sick man to drink. She also sent him word that their brother would not die, as it was the will of God that he should help to spread the devotion to the Sacred Heart. The water in which the writing had been dipped was given to the sick man, and he had no sooner drunk it than he got well. He thenceforth led a holy life, and helped very much to spread the devotion to the Sacred Heart. Chrysostom soon afterwards began to build a chapel in honour of the Sacred Heart, and his brother the priest founded a Mass to be said there on the first Friday of every month. Margaret Mary wrote the following letter to her brother a few days after his miraculous restoration to health :

" January 22, 1687. It is a sweet consolation to me, dearest brother, that the goodness of the Sacred Heart of our Lord Jesus Christ condescends to make His will agree with ours by keeping you yet a little longer here below in this land of wretchedness and tears, where, we must confess with the Apostle, everything is vanity and affliction of spirit, except loving and serving God alone. I thought that I had already spoken to you of this newly established devotion, but, as you have not given me an answer, I did not know whether what I said was pleasing to you; but it seems

to me that there is no shorter road to perfection, nor
a surer means of salvation than to consecrate oneself
wholly to this Divine Heart; to offer to It all the
homage of love, honour, and praise of which we are
capable. This is the reason why you are pledged to
it, and I hope to speak more fully about it when I
shall have the happiness to see you, should it be the
good pleasure of God to grant me that consolation."

Margaret Mary wrote as follows to her elder brother
Chrysostom : " You could not, my dear brother, do
me a greater favour than by giving me such pleasant
news about the good dispositions which the Sacred
Heart fosters in your soul. I did not dare to say any
more to you about it, for devotions are never solid
unless they come from the movement of divine grace.
But you must, without fail, do what you have undertaken. You will give me one of the greatest pleasures
which I can have in this mortal life if you do it ; for
nothing can give me so much joy as to see the Sacred
Heart of our Lord loved, honoured, and glorified.
I hope that my brother the priest will not refuse to
help to the best of his ability towards an object
which is so greatly for the glory of the Sacred Heart,
and which will draw down many graces upon you and
upon your family." She wrote on this subject to Mother
de Saumaise : " It is my brother the mayor who is
building the chapel at Bois Sainte Marie. He has
also ordered a painting like ours, which he intends to
place there. My brother the priest is also founding
a perpetual Mass, to be said on the first Friday of the

month. I tell this to you in order that you may thank the Sacred Heart, which has inspired them to do it; for I did not speak to them about it, although I would have gladly done so, for I would much rather that it came from themselves. You cannot think what a change the Sacred Heart has worked in the family. They have assured me that they would be willing to give the last drop of their blood to uphold and to prosper this holy devotion."

Margaret Mary was about to have the happiest day of her life—a day of spiritual gladness after many years of weary waiting for the fulfilment of her wishes for the triumph of the Sacred Heart. The chapel which the Visitation nuns of Paray had built in their convent garden was solemnly dedicated to the Sacred Heart of Jesus, September 7th, in the year 1688. The priests of the town and country, followed by a throng of the faithful, came in the afternoon in devout procession from the parish church to the Visitation convent, and, entering the enclosure, performed the ceremony of dedication. Margaret Mary meanwhile remained kneeling, during the two hours of the ceremony, before the picture of the Sacred Heart which was upon the altar, motionless and lost in ecstasy; and, although many stood near and gazed at her with reverence, nobody dared to speak to her, for she who formerly had been considered to be a hypocrite and possessed by the devil was now known to be a saint. Margaret Mary declared, when the ceremony of the dedication was over, that the Lord was so well pleased with the trouble that Mother Melin had taken to have a sanctuary built wherein His Sacred Heart might be worshipped that He had promised, as a reward, that she should die making an act of pure love.

CHAPTER XV

HE Visitation community at Dijon celebrated a festival in their convent chapel,
and Mass was offered up in honour of the
Sacred Heart, on the first Friday of
February, in the year 1689. When Margaret Mary
heard of this celebration, she wrote as follows to
Mother de Saumaise : " Oh, what happiness for you
and for all who help towards it, for they thereby draw
down the friendship and the everlasting blessings of
this amiable Heart, and gain a powerful Protector for
our fatherland ! A no less mighty power was needed
to turn away the gall and severity of the righteous
wrath of God on account of so many crimes which are
committed ; but I hope that this Divine Heart will
become for it an unfailing fountain of mercy. It
seeks to establish Its kingdom amongst us, and to
bestow Its precious graces of sanctification and salvation more plentifully upon us. There is one thing
which gives me great comfort—it is that I hope that,
in exchange for the bitterness which this Divine Heart

has endured in the palaces of the great during the ill-treatment of His Passion, this devotion will find an entrance there with splendour in the course of time. Continue, therefore, courageously what you have begun for Its glory by establishing this kingdom. The Sacred Heart shall reign despite Satan and all whom he stirs up to oppose It. But now is the time to work and to suffer in silence, as It has done for love of us."

The picture of the Sacred Heart was thenceforth exposed for veneration in the convent choir at Dijon on the first Friday of every month, and the Religious of that community were accustomed to spend the whole of that day praying before the picture. There was a public solemnity after Easter, by permission of the bishop, in honour of the Sacred Heart, in the convent chapel. Mass was sung by the Chapter, and the Blessed Sacrament was exposed throughout the day. Sister Johanna Mary Joly, who was a nun of that community, wrote a mass in French in honour of the Sacred Heart, and the confessor of the convent translated it into Latin. This mass was sent to the Convent of the Visitation at Rome, together with a petition to the Holy See for permission to have it sung publicly in every church on the Friday after the Octave of Corpus Christi. Margaret Mary wrote: " I think that I would die happy if you obtained permission for the mass in honour of the Adorable Heart of Jesus ". The Holy See, however, answered that it was neces-sary that the devotion should first be publicly established in the diocese with permission of the bishop.

Margaret Mary fell into an ecstasy on the Friday after the Octave day of Corpus Christi, June 17, in the year 1689, and on that day she wrote these words to Mother de Saumaise: " My dear Mother, are we not at length quite consumed with the flames of this Divine Heart, after having received so many graces, which are so many burning flames of its pure love. It will reign, this amiable Heart, in spite of Satan and his followers. This word overwhelms me with gladness. But to be able to tell you the great graces and blessings which will be bestowed upon those who shall obtain most honour and glory for it, is what I cannot say in the way that He has made it known to me. He has then shown me the devotion of His Divine Heart as a beautiful tree which He has destined from all eternity to be sown and to take root amid our Institute, in order afterwards to spread its branches in the houses which compose it, so that everyone may gather its fruits at will and according to her taste. But He wishes that the daughters of the Visitation should plentifully give the fruits of this sacred tree to all those who may desire to eat of them, wishing thus to restore many to life by withdrawing them from the way of perdition, and to destroy the kingdom of Satan in the souls of men, in order to establish therein that of His love.

" But He does not wish to stop short at that : He has still greater designs, which can be fulfilled only by His omnipotence, which can do all that He wishes. He wishes then, as it seems to me, to enter with pomp and splendour into the house of princes and of kings, in order to be there honoured as much as He was dishonoured, despised, and humiliated, during His Passion, and in order to receive as much pleasure at beholding the nobles of the earth bowed down and lowly before Him as He experienced bitterness at beholding Himself abased at their feet. The following are the words which I heard on this subject : ' Make known to the eldest son of My Sacred Heart—speaking of our King—that as his temporal birth was obtained through devotion to the merits of my holy Childhood, in like manner he will obtain his birth of grace and of everlasting glory by his consecration to My adorable Heart, which de- sires to conquer his, and through him, that of the nobles of the earth. It desires to reign in his palace, to be painted on his standards, and to be engraven upon his arms, in order to make them triumph over all his foes.' "

Margaret Mary knew that her mission from God would not be fulfilled until she had endeavoured to lead Louis XIV. to swear fealty, and to consecrate both himself and his kingdom to the Sacred Heart of Jesus Christ. She therefore wrote the following declaration in the month of August, in the year 1689 :

" The Eternal Father, desiring to make amends for the bitterness and the sufferings which the adorable

Heart of His Divine Son received in the house of the princes of the earth, amid the humiliations and ill-treatment of His Passion, wishes to establish His kingdom in the heart of our great monarch, whom He desires to use for the fulfilment of His design, which is to have an edifice built wherein should be the picture of His Divine Heart, in order to receive there the consecration and the homage of the king and of his whole court.

"This Divine Heart, moreover, desires to become the protector and the defender of his sacred person against all his foes. He has therefore chosen him as His faithful friend to obtain permission from the Holy Apostolic See for the Mass, and to obtain all the other privileges which ought to accompany the devotion of this Divine Heart. It is through this Divine Heart that He desires to bestow the treasures of His graces and of salvation by pouring out His blessings upon all his undertakings, by giving a happy success to his arms, and by making him victorious over the wickedness of his enemies."

Margaret Mary sought to have this declaration on the part of Jesus Christ presented to the King of France, through means of his confessor, Père de la Chaise; but she acknowledged that the work was difficult, both on account of the hindrances which Satan would put in the way, and also on account of the hindrances which God would allow to be put in order to show forth His power. Her words, however, most probably reached Louis XIV.; but the wicked King gave no heed to the loving invitation of the Sacred Heart of Jesus Christ.

Father Croiset, of the Society of Jesus, came from Lyons to visit Margaret Mary, and she spoke to him with such wisdom and fervour that he thought her to be inspired by God. When he returned home he endeavoured to inspire the youths who studied at the Jesuit College at Lyons with a great love and devotion for the Sacred Heart, but he had no thought of writing a book. Margaret Mary however said : " The devotion to the Sacred Heart of Jesus will be made known everywhere through means of a book by Father Croiset the Jesuit," and it was about it that she wrote as follows to a friend : " I must tell you something which is for the glory of the Divine Heart, and it will give you cause for blessing it. I had given one of the Dijon books to a lady from Lyons. She gave it to a young father to read. Having shown it to his pupils at Lyons, they took such a fancy to it that they made a great many copies both of the litanies and of the prayers, which they recited very devoutly. And these children having shown them to others, these also got such a great devotion to them, that, as they were not able to make copies enough, they determined to have one of these books printed, offering to bear the expense. And a young workman was so anxious to take upon himself the expense, that they had to yield to his devotion. And when he went for that purpose to one of the chief booksellers of Lyons, he too felt himself so moved with love of this

Divine Heart, that he undertook out of devotion to publish it at his own expense, which caused a holy combat between the youth and himself; but he, having at length gained his point, got the book of the Sacred Heart, and went to one of his friends to have it written more fully, and a holy Religious took charge of it. And they have newly reprinted them, and they are very beautiful and well bound, and their sale has been so great that they have reprinted them since the 19th of June, and now on the 21st of August there are no longer any left, and they are therefore going to reprint them for the third time."

This book spread through France and was translated into Italian, and Margaret Mary was so delighted that she wrote, in October of the year 1689, the following enthusiastic letter to a friend : " What a consolation to hear of the happy progress of this beloved devotion. We hear from Lyons that it is almost a miracle to see how everybody gives himself with fervour and eagerness to it. We have been told of three or four towns where these books are about to be printed, and Marseilles is one of them, and a thousand have been taken there. And out of the twenty-seven Religious houses which are in that city, there is not one which has not taken up this devotion with so much zeal, that some build altars in its honour, and some build chapels." The people of Paray were not behindhand in showing veneration and love to the Sacred Heart, and it became the custom there to make novenas with lighted candles in its honour. Devotion to the

Heart of Jesus Christ which had been planted through means of Margaret Mary grew apace, and the seeds were scattered broadcast throughout the length and breadth of France by means of books written in its praise. "Their voice went forth into every land, and their words unto the ends of the earth." Margaret Mary waited many weary years until it grew above the ground, for God wished it to strike deep root. And as she wrote: "It insinuated itself slowly by the sweet unction of charity into the hearts which were destined to receive it, like oil and costly balm, which flows gently and whose perfume spreads around".

CHAPTER XVI.

ARGARET MARY meanwhile went forward as a shining light growing into perfect day ; a great calm had been made in her heart ; her life flowed smoothly onwards, and her days were beautiful and serene like the soft beams of the setting sun in a rich and lonely valley. Her thoughts and words and works were sweet strains of music that went up to heaven, and mingled with the melody of the angels as they sang around the throne of God ; and she was a living likeness of the Sacred Heart of Jesus Christ. The nuns, the novices, and the convent children looked upon her as a saint, and the workmen who came within the enclosure gazed at her with awe. She no longer, however, showed outwardly the wonderful work of God in her soul, but led henceforth a lowly and a hidden life, for her mission upon earth had been fulfilled. Saint Jane de Chantal once prayed earnestly to God that He would hide the life of the Religious of the Order of the Visitation of Holy Mary in

Himself with Jesus Christ, and whilst Saint Francis of Sales was one day saying Holy Mass for that intention, she learned that her prayer had been heard, and that God would bestow upon her Order a great gift of the hidden life and the graces of His Son hidden in Himself, to be manifested only in eternity, and that if some wonderful works should be done in some souls it should be as a homage to the Transfiguration and the wonderful works of Jesus Christ. Margaret Mary, hitherto, had shown forth the wonder-working life of the Son of God, but she now once more led like Him a lowly and a hidden life—a life hidden with Him in God.

Her sufferings indeed still weighed heavily upon her, but she loved the cross and was always full of gladness. She wrote to the mother superior at Moulins: " How good it is to be always suffering and at length to die upon the cross, crushed beneath the load of every kind of affliction, misfortune, contempt, abandonment, and humiliation. The cross is a precious balm which loses its perfume before God when it is made known. Let us never grow weary of suffering for we cannot love without suffering. Oh, how sweet the cross is at all times and in all places. Let us ever cling lovingly to it, not minding of what wood it is made nor how it is hewn, for nothing so unites us to the Sacred Heart of Jesus as the cross, which is the most precious proof of His love."

Her work upon earth was finished, and she yearned wistfully to end her exile, to forsake her prison, and to fly to her heavenly home. She learned by a supernatural light in the month of July, 1690, that the day of her death was drawing nigh, and she got permission to make a spiritual retreat of forty days as a preparation for it. She said to the nuns when her retreat was over that she should die soon, as she was a hindrance to the spreading of the devotion to the Sacred Heart; but they gave no heed to her words. She, however, got a slight fever at the beginning of the month of October, in the year 1690; and although the doctor made little of it, this was, as she well knew, her last sickness. She said one day to a young nun who was standing by her bedside, " I shall die of this sickness, and we shall not be long together; I shall die in your arms ". But the young sister was frightened at the thought of death, and said that she could not give her that help. The dying saint, however, assured her that it would be as she had foretold. The young nun, although she was unwilling to assist her when she should be dying, nevertheless loved to linger by her bedside speaking of holy things with her, for they loved each other very much, and she one day said to the dying saint : " Mother, you are suffering a great deal," but Margaret Mary answered : " I do not suffer enough, the short time which remains is too valuable not to profit by it ; I suffer much but not enough to satisfy my wishes ; and I find such delight in living and dying upon the cross, that, although I desire to enjoy God, still I would be more pleased to stay as I am

12

until the day of judgment, should it be the will of God ".

Margaret Mary was very patient, humble, and obedient during her illness, and was always united to God. She was full of joy at the thought that her last hour was drawing nigh, for she wistfully yearned to leave this barren land to go to her heavenly home. She especially wished to join the heavenly choirs who ever sing the praises of God ; for, to use the words of Saint Francis of Sales, not being able to sing or to hear the divine praises to her liking, she had an unutterable desire to be freed from the bonds of this life in order to go to the other life where the Heavenly Beloved is so perfectly praised ; and these desires, having taken possession of her heart, became so strong, that banishing all other desires, they caused a disgust for all earthly things, and made her soul languishing and lovesick ; like a heavenly nightingale shut up in the cage of her body, where she could not sing at will the praises of her eternal love, knowing that she could better trill and sing her delicious song if she might gain her freedom, and the society of the other nightingales amid the gay and flowery hills of the land of the blessed.

Margaret Mary asked for Holy Viaticum on the morning of October 16, but as she did not seem to be very ill she was allowed only to receive Holy Communion in the usual way. She broke forth into burning words of love and thanksgiving as soon as she beheld the Blessed Sacrament, and she often said

during that day, "Oh, what a happiness it is to love
God! Let us love God! Let us love God! but
perfectly." She wasted away like incense upon the
fire of divine love. A cloud, however, overshadowed
her mind for a moment towards evening, and she
trembled, and, clasping her crucifix with her hands, she
cried out with fear, "Mercy: my God! mercy!" but
peace and calmness soon came back, and her deathlike face wore thenceforth a sweet smile which showed
forth the gladness of her heart. The Litanies of the
Sacred Heart and of the Blessed Virgin were recited
by the nuns at her bedside, and special prayers were
also said to Saint Joseph, to Saint Francis of Sales,
and to her Guardian Angel. She spent most of that
evening without speaking, but at nightfall she suddenly
entreated the young sister whom she loved so much to
burn all her writings.

The last day of her holy life at length dawned.
She became very weak early in the morning, and the
doctor was sent for, but he said that she was not in
danger of death. She answered: "You will see".
When she heard that the mother superior had sent
word of her illness to her family, she expressed
unwillingness to see them, saying, "Let us die and
sacrifice everything to God". She often spoke during
the day to the sister who stayed by her bedside of the
wonderful love of God towards mankind, and she
from time to time broke forth into these words: "I
shall sing the mercies of the Lord for ever"—"What
do I desire in heaven or on earth but Thee alone, my

God?" She began to burn with fever towards evening and could hardly breathe, and she said to the sisters who were supporting her in their arms on the chair on which she was seated: "I burn! Oh, if it were with divine love! But I never loved God perfectly. Ask forgiveness for me, and love Him with your whole heart in order to make atonement for all the moments when I failed to do it."

The doctor was again sent for, but he again said that there was no danger, and when she asked for Holy Viaticum he said that she must wait until the following day. The Religious then went away to their work, and she was left alone with only one sister. She asked this sister whether she thought that she should last much longer, and the sister answered that she thought that she could not live beyond the following day. Margaret Mary then cried out: "O Lord, when wilt Thou take me from this place of evil? I have rejoiced in what has been said to me; we shall go into the house of the Lord. Yes, I hope that through the love of the Heart of Jesus Christ we shall go into the house of the Lord, and that it shall be soon." She then begged the sister who was watching by her bedside to fetch the mother superior as soon as she saw her agony begin, and to ask her to have the Litanies of the Sacred Heart and of the Blessed Virgin said for her.

Her agony began as soon as she had spoken these words, and the mother superior and the community

were at once summoned to her bedside. She then
spoke to them with her weak voice, as they were
gathered in the room around her, and earnestly entreated them to love God with their whole heart; and
she promised that she would remember their kindness
and affection towards herself when she should be allowed to appear in the presence of God. She begged
the mother superior to burn all her writings, and she
asked one of the nuns to write to Rev. Father Rolin,
her former confessor, begging him to burn all her
letters and her writings. She then warned the mother
superior that it was time to give her the Sacrament of
Extreme Unction. The priest, therefore, anointed her.
She was most recollected and lost in God during this
impressive ceremony; and as soon as he had finished
the fourth anointing she uttered the holy name Jesus
and fell dead, as she had foretold, into the arms of
two young sisters, her former novices, who had rushed
to help her when she had raised herself up in order to
be anointed. She died in the evening of October 17,
in the year 1690, at the age of forty-three years; and
her face became so lovely after death that the nuns
stayed as long as they could in the room where her
body was laid out. Everyone in the convent and in
the town spoke of her as a saint, and prayed to her.

The townsfolk thronged the convent chapel at dawn
the following morning, as soon as the door had been
opened; and two nuns were busy the whole day from
early morning until evening touching the holy body of
the saint with the beads, medals, and crucifixes given

to them for that purpose. Her body was buried that evening with great solemnity in the convent choir. The nuns wept that night when they thought of their want of esteem and love for their saintly sister whilst she dwelt amongst them ; but they were filled with gladness when they thought of her holy life, and of their firm hope that her spotless soul had entered through the golden gates of the heavenly city, and was already joining in the songs of angels and saints before the throne of God.

CHAPTER XVII

ARGARET MARY was dead : the silver cord of her life was broken ; the earthen pitcher lay shattered at the fountain ; her body had gone back to the dust whence it had come ; and her pure soul had gone back to God who gave it. She no longer roamed weary and foot-sore through this bleak and sinful world, far from her heavenly home, but she was enjoying the spiritual wealth which by her good works she had treasured up for herself in heaven, where her momentary and light tribulations had worked an eternal weight of glory. She had sown in sorrows and now reaped in joy a plentiful harvest of everlasting happiness. Her watchings before the Blessed Sacrament in the little chapel at Corcheval, her prayers and penances in the lonely glen at Lhautecour, her heroic patience in the home of her childhood, her sacrifice of the glittering hopes of earthly happiness and of the bright blossoms of youthful pleasures, her faithfulness to God amid the turmoil and temptations of the world, her unceasing

devotions, sacrifices, and penances in the cloister, and, above all, her unwavering and burning love for the Sacred Heart of Jesus Christ, were now rewarded a hundredfold on that bright and happy day, when, having passed safely over the wide and pathless sea of this world, she reached the eternal shore and entered into the kingdom of heaven to possess for ever its unfading glory, to follow the Lamb whithersoever He goeth, and to sing the new canticle before the throne of God.

Margaret Mary was revered upon earth whilst she was glorified in heaven, and a widespread devotion suddenly sprang up towards the Saint of the Sacred Heart. Men and women hastened from far and near and thronged around her tomb; and many who had come to Paray to do her honour and to invoke her intercession were rewarded for their devotion with wonderful miracles. Some who for many months were bowed down with sickness regained their health when they prayed to her; some who were tossed about at the mercy of the wild waves of this wicked world amidst shoals and rocks once again were filled with hope and happiness as they knelt before her shrine; and some by calling on her for help were brought back almost from the grave.

The devotion to the Sacred Heart spread wonderfully throughout the world as soon as Margaret Mary was dead. A small book containing a short sketch of her life, which was published by Father Croiset, helped very much to make known this holy devotion.

The Feast of the Sacred Heart was solemnly celebrated
in many dioceses, and more than thirty confraternities
were established in its honour within thirty years of
her death. This great devotion thus spread throughout Christendom, as Margaret Mary had foretold, in
spite of the relentless opposition of the proud and
heartless Jansenists and the calumnies and mockery
of unbelievers. The sudden ceasing of the plague
at Marseilles through the devotion of the inhabitants
of that city to the Sacred Heart caused an enthusiastic
outburst of devotion to it throughout the length and
breadth of France. The plague was brought from the
East by a ship in the summer of the year 1720, and
before four months were over 40,000 citizens had
been swept away by it. The churches were closed,
the bells were silent, and no sound was heard in the
streets save the sobs and groans of the plague-stricken.
Dead bodies lay in heaps in the middle of the streets,
food for dogs; and old men and women, and even
children, lay dying upon the doorsteps of the houses
whence they had been thrust by their affrighted families.
The wealthy and most of the magistrates fled from the
city of the dead, and the bishop and his clergy alone
stayed to help and comfort the sick and dying; but
250 priests soon died martyrs of charity. The bishop
then bethought him of the Sacred Heart of Jesus
Christ, and he resolved to put his hope in that loving
Heart, and to seek help from it. On the first day of
November the long silent bells once more boomed
slowly and sadly from the towers and steeples, break-

ing the deathlike stillness of the doomed city, and at
early morning the bishop and clergy, followed by the
faithful, went forth barefoot, with ropes round their
necks and with crucifixes in their hands, and walked
in procession through the streets from the president's
palace to the public square, and there the bishop,
kneeling amidst his weeping flock, solemnly consecrated his diocese to the Sacred Heart of Jesus Christ.
The wrath of God was appeased. The angel of death
sheathed his sword. The number of deaths daily
decreased, and hope again dawned in the hearts of
the citizens. The plague ceased altogether after
Easter, and the bells once more rang out a merry
peal, and the churches once more were thronged with
worshippers, who gave heartfelt thanks to the loving
Heart of Christ for Its mercy towards them.

The devotion to the Sacred Heart was solemnly
approved by the Holy See in the year 1765, and the
bishops of Poland, the Archconfraternity of the
Sacred Heart at Rome, and shortly afterwards the
Visitation Order, got permission from Clement XIII.
to celebrate the Feast of the Sacred Heart with a
special office and mass. Pius VI. extended this
privilege to many dioceses and religious orders, and
enriched the devotion with very many indulgences ;
and Pius IX. ordered the Feast of the Sacred Heart to
be celebrated on the first Friday after the Octave of
Corpus Christi in every church throughout the world,
"in order to move the faithful anew to love, and to
make a return of love to the wounded Heart of Him

who loved us, and washed us from our sins in His blood". The Catholic Church was consecrated to the Sacred Heart of Jesus Christ by Pius IX., in the year 1875, and thus the devotion which was revealed through the lowly nun of Paray-le-Monial prevailed, as she had foretold, in every land and nation.

Leo XIII., in the year 1889, raised the Feast of the Sacred Heart to the rite of Double of the First Class. "Two centuries have well-nigh gone by since the faithful began, with daily increasing devotion, to venerate, under the symbol of the Sacred Heart, the chief benefits of the love of our Divine Redeemer; and many bishops, from every part of the world, have, in the name of their clergy and people, often petitioned our Holy Father Pope Leo XIII. to raise the Feast of the Sacred Heart to the rite of Double of First Class. The Holy Father, who has nothing more at heart than that the faithful should grow in grace and in the knowledge of our Lord Jesus Christ, gladly received their petition, having especially in view that the faithful should find refuge and defence, in spite of the working of wickedness, in this most saving devotion, and that, enflamed with burning love of the most loving Redeemer, they should offer Him a worthy homage of praise and expiation, and, at the same time, should most fervently beg the divine mercy for the growth of faith and the peace and safety of the Christian people. The Holy Father, being moved by these considerations, has, by special favour and privilege, decreed that the Feast of the Sacred Heart of Jesus be celebrated throughout the world as a Double of the First Class."

Margaret Mary was declared Blessed by Pius IX. in the year 1864; and the Holy Father stated, in the Brief of Beatification, that she had been "chosen by God to establish this salutary devotion, and to spread it far and wide amongst men; and that she had proved herself worthy of this high office and mission by her stainless life and by the constant practice of every virtue". An office and mass were allowed to be said in her honour, together with special prayers, in the diocese of Autun and in the convents of the Visitation Order, and October 17th was appointed as her feast day. We hope that the higher honour of canonisation may be bestowed upon this great servant of the Sacred Heart, and that her festival, with office and mass, may soon be extended to the whole Catholic Church.

I.—Reparation of Honour.

O Divine Heart of Jesus, boundless source of love and goodness, how much do I regret that I have so often forgotten Thee, and so little loved Thee. O Sacred Heart, Thou dost deserve the love and the devotion of all those hearts which Thou hast infinitely loved and cherished; yet Thou dost receive from them nothing but coldness and ingratitude; and especially from my unfaithful heart, which justly merits Thy anger. But as Thou art a Heart of love Thou art also full of goodness, from which I hope for forgiveness and reconciliation. Alas, O Divine Heart, I acknowledge with the deepest sorrow my too great lukewarmness, and confess the unrighteousness of my wicked heart in robbing Thee unjustly of the love which is due to Thee alone, in order to appropriate it to myself or to some other earthly object. O most gentle Heart, if the sorrow and the shame of a heart

[1] *The Sacred Hearts of Jesus and Mary*, by Rev. J. A. Krebs, C.SS.R.

which sees its error can make atonement to Thee, forgive my heart, for its want of love and of fidelity has put it in this state. Alas! what could it expect but hatred and punishment unless it hoped for everything from Thy mercy. O Heart of my God, most holy Heart, 'Heart to which alone the pardon of sinners belongs, have mercy, I beseech Thee, upon this wretched heart of mine. All its faculties unite to make, with the utmost humility, a reparation of honour to Thee for all its wanderings and infidelities. Oh, how could I have refused so long to give Thee my heart, for Thou alone art its rightful owner. I am sorry, with my whole heart, for having strayed so far from Thee and from Thy love, from the fountain of all good—in a word, from the Heart of my Jesus, who, without having any need of me, first sought for and loved me. O most adorable Heart, how could I have thus treated Thee, on whose love and goodness I am wholly dependent; and if Thou didst withdraw either the one or the other for a moment, I should be brought to the greatest wretchedness, or be utterly destroyed. O loving Heart, how infinite has been Thy goodness to have borne so long with my ingratitude; there remains nothing but for Thy mercy to forgive my wretched and inconstant heart. O Heart of my Jesus, I now consecrate and give Thee all my love and my heart; I give both to Thee for ever, but with a profound feeling of shame on account of having so long refused Thee that which was Thine own. O divine Heart, Thou wouldst prove to me the

excess of Thy love by making me capable of loving
Thee, and, alas ! I have profited so badly of this
opportunity of meriting Thy favours.   I am truly
sorry ; and I most humbly beseech Thee, O Heart of
my Jesus, to renew my heart, hitherto so faithless.
Grant that it may be bound to Thee henceforth by
the bonds of love, and may draw so much nearer to
Thee as it has hitherto wandered far from Thee ; and,
as Thou art my Creator, be also, I beseech Thee, my
everlasting reward.   Amen.

II.—CONFIDENCE IN THE SACRED HEART.

O most Sacred and Divine Heart of Jesus, from the
abyss of my nothingness I prostrate myself in Thy
presence in order to give Thee all the homage of love,
adoration, and praise which I am able ; to lay before
Thee all my wants, by making known to Thee, as to
my best friend, all my wretchedness, my poverty, my
failings, and my lukewarmness—in a word, all the
wounds of my soul—beseeching Thee to have pity and
compassion upon me, and to help me, according to the
greatness of Thy mercies.   O Heart of love, I beseech
Thee, by all that can move Thee, to bestow on me
this grace to save my soul, and the souls of all those
who, like myself, are in danger of being lost for ever.
O most merciful Heart, do not allow me to perish
amid the deluge of my sins.   Do with me what Thou
wilt, if only I may love Thee for all eternity.   I have
placed all my hope in Thee ; do not cast me off for
ever.   I call upon Thee ; I invoke Thee as the

sovereign remedy of all my evils, the chief of which is sin. O destroy this in me, I beseech Thee, and grant me forgiveness for all the sins which I have committed during my lifetime, for which I am most heartily sorry. O Sacred Heart, make me, and all those hearts which are able to love Thee, feel and experience Thy supreme power; I beg this grace for my parents, my friends, and for all those who have been recommended to my prayers, or who pray for me, and for whom I am specially bound to pray. I beseech Thee to help them according to the necessities of each. O most loving Heart, soften hardened sinners, and comfort the souls in Purgatory; be the safe refuge of the dying, and the consolation of the afflicted and of the needy. O Heart of love, be, lastly, my all in all, but especially be the haven of rest for my soul at the hour of my death. Yes, receive me, at that moment, into the bosom of Thy mercy. Amen.

THE ABERDEEN UNIVERSITY PRESS.

SELECTION

FROM

BURNS & OATES'

Catalogue

OF

PUBLICATIONS.

LONDON: BURNS AND OATES, Lᴅ.

28 ORCHARD ST., W., & 63 PATERNOSTER ROW, E.C.

NEW YORK: 12 EAST 17ᴛʜ STREET.

1891.

NEW BOOKS JUST OUT.

Saint Ignatius Loyola and The Early Jesuits. By STEWART
ROSE. With more than 100 Illustrations by H.W. and H.C.
Brewer and L. Wain. The whole brought out under the
immediate superintendence of the Rev. W. H. Eyre, S.J.
Super Royal 8vo. Handsomely bound in Cloth, extra gilt. Price
15s. *net.* (Very suitable for a Prize or Gift.)

The Letters of the late Father George Porter, S.J., ARCH-
BISHOP OF BOMBAY. Demy 8vo. Cloth, 7s. 6d.

Acts of the English Martyrs, hitherto unpublished. By the
Rev. JOHN H. POLLEN, S.J. With a Preface by the Rev. JOHN
MORRIS, S.J., Quarterly Series (Vol. 75). Crown 8vo, cloth, in
two styles, 7s. 6d.

The Christian Virgin in her Family and in the World. Her
Virtues and her Mission at the Present Time. Handsomely
bound in blue cloth, leather back, gilt top, 6s.
"The aim of the present book is to show how all those who,
whether from choice or necessity, are led to live with their families
or alone in the world may, by consecrating and sanctifying their
state, lead a life, not only useful and meritorious, but amiable
and pleasant to themselves and to society in general. The
translation bears the imprimatur of the Cardinal Archbishop of
Westminster."—*Tablet.*

The Blind Apostle and **A Heroine of Charity.** By the late
KATHLEEN O'MEARA. With a Preface by the Cardinal Archbishop of Westminster. Vol. 3, "Bells of the Sanctuary" Series.
Crown 8vo, cloth, gilt, 4s. 6d.
"Mgr. de Ségur's (the Blind Apostle) life is a story of our own
time, and tells of the heroic courage in which, in spite of total
blindness, he laboured for thirteen years, preaching, hearing confessions, and even contributing book after book to popular Catholic
literature. Madame Legras (the Heroine of Charity) was the noble-
hearted woman to whom St. Vincent de Paul entrusted the work
of founding the order of the Sisters of Charity."—*Catholic Times.*

My Time, and what I've done with it. An Autobiography.
By F. C. BURNAND. With Portrait of the Author. Crown 8vo,
cloth, 5s.
"Interweaves with a partly fictitious plot Mr. Burnand's impressions
of his boyhood and youth, especially of that period which he spent
at 'Holyshade' (Eton), 'Tudor College' (Cowbridge), and 'St.
Bede's' (Cuddleston). Each of these experiences yields to Mr.
Burnand a little budget of portraits of the ruling powers. Dr. Keate,
Canon Liddon, Bishop Wilberforce, and other celebrities, living
and dead, are recognizable under their disguises. The author of
'Happy Thoughts' is an acute analyst of the sensations and unconscious reflections of boyhood as well as of manhood. For various
reasons, then, this volume will be found entertaining."—*Times.*

Immediately.

The Autobiography of Archbishop Ullathorne. With Selec-
tions from his letters. By AUGUSTA THEODOSIA DRANE.

Ireland and St. Patrick. A Study of the Saint's Character, and
of the results of his Apostolate. By the Rev. W. B. MORRIS, of
the Oratory.

Succat; or, Sixty Years of the Life of St. Patrick. By the Very
Rev. Mgr. ROBERT GRADWELL.

SELECTION

FROM

BURNS AND OATES' CATALOGUE OF PUBLICATIONS.

—⟶⟶⟶✦✦⟵⟵⟵—

ALLIES, T. W. (K.C. S.G.)

Formation of Christendom. Vols. I., II., and III.,
(all out of print.)   .   .   .   .
Church and State as seen in the Formation of Christen-
dom, 8vo, pp. 472, cloth   .   (out of print.)
The Throne of the Fisherman, built by the Carpenter's
Son, the Root, the Bond, and the Crown of Christ-
endom. Demy 8vo   .   .   .   .   .   ;   0 10 6
The Holy See and the Wandering of the Nations.
Demy 8vo. 0 10 6
Peter's Rock in Mohammed's Flood. Demy 8vo.   .   0 10 6

"It would be quite superfluous at this hour of the day to recommend
Mr. Allies' writings to English Catholics. Those of our readers who
remember the article on his writings in the *Katholik*, know that
he is esteemed in Germany as one of our foremost writers."—
Dublin Review.

ALLIES, MARY.

Leaves from St. John Chrysostom, With introduction
by T. W. Allies, K.C.S.G. Crown 8vo, cloth   .   0   6   0

"Miss Allies 'Leaves' are delightful reading; the English is re-
markably pure and graceful; page after page reads as if it were
original. No commentator, Catholic or Protestant, has ever surpassed St. John Chrysostom in the knowledge of Holy Scripture,
and his learning was of a kind which is of service now as it was at
the time when the inhabitants of a great city hung on his words."—
Tablet.

ALLNATT, C. F. B.

Cathedra Petri. Third and Enlarged Edition. Cloth   0   6   0
"Invaluable to the controversialist and the theologian, and most
useful for educated men inquiring after truth or anxious to know
the positive testimony of Christian antiquity in favour of Papal
claims."—*Month.*

Which is the True Church? Fifth Edition   .   .   0   1   4
The Church and the Sects .   .   .   .   .   :   0   1   0
Ditto,   Ditto.   Second Series. .   .   .   0   1   6

ANNUS SANCTUS:

Hymns of the Church for the Ecclesiastical Year.
Translated from the Sacred Offices by various
Authors, with Modern, Original, and other Hymns,
and an Appendix of Earlier Versions. Selected and
Arranged by ORBY SHIPLEY, M.A.
Popular edition, in two parts   .   .   each   1   0   0
In stiff boards   0   3   6
Plain Cloth, lettered   0   5   0
Edition de luxe 0 10   6

ANSWERS TO ATHEISTS : OR NOTES ON
Ingersoll. By the Rev. A. Lambert, (over 100,000 copies
sold in America). Ninth edition. Paper. . . . £0 o 6
  Cloth . .   .   .   o 1 o

B. N.
The Jesuits : their Foundation and History. 2 vols.
  crown 8vo, cloth, red edges . .   .   .   .   o 15 o
"The book is just what it professes to be—*a popular history*,
drawn from well-known sources," &c.—*Month.*

BAKER, VEN. FATHER AUGUSTIN.
Holy Wisdom ; or, Directions for the Prayer of Contemplation, &c. Extracted from Treatises written
by the Ven. Father F. Augustin Baker, O.S.B., and
edited by Abbot Sweeney, D.D. Beautifully bound
in half leather . .   .   .   o 6 o
"We earnestly recommend this most beautiful work to all our
readers. We are sure that every community will use it as a constant
manual. If any persons have friends in convents, we cannot conceive
a better present they can make them, or a better claim they can have
on their prayers, than by providing them with a copy."—*Weekly
Register.*

BORROMEO, LIFE OF ST. CHARLES.
From the Italian of Peter Guissano. 2 vols. . .   o 15 o
"A standard work, which has stood the test of succeeding ages; it
is certainly the finest work on St. Charles in an English dress."—
Tablet.

BOWDEN, REV. H. S. (of the Oratory) Edited by.
Dante's Divina Commedia : Its scope and value.
From the German of FRANCIS HETTINGER, D.D.
With an engraving of Dante. Crown 8vo . .   o 10 6
"All that Venturi attempted to do has been now approached with
far greater power and learning by Dr. Hettinger, who, as the author
of the 'Apologie des Christenthums,' and as a great Catholic theolo-
gian, is eminently well qualified for the task he has undertaken."—
The Saturday Review.
Natural Religion. Being Vol. I. of Dr. Hettinger's
Evidences of Christianity. Edited, with an Intro-
duction on Certainty, by the Rev. H. S. Bowden.
Crown 8vo, cloth . .   .   .   .   .   o 7 6
            (Other volumes in preparation.)
"As an able statement of the Catholic Doctrine of Certitude, and
a defence, from the Romanist point of view, of the truth of Christian-
ity, it was well worth while translating Dr. Franz Hettinger's
'Apologie des Christenthums,' of which the first part is now published."—*Scotsman.*

BRIDGETT, REV. T. E. (C.SS.R.).
Discipline of Drink . . .   .   o 3 6
"The historical information with which the book abounds gives
evidence of deep research and patient study, and imparts a per-
manent interest to the volume, which will elevate it to a position
of authority and importance enjoyed by few of its compeers."—*The
Arrow.*
Our Lady's Dowry ; how England Won that Title.
New and Enlarged Edition. .   .   .   .   o 5 o
"This book is the ablest vindication of Catholic devotion to Our
Lady, drawn from tradition, that we know of in the English lan-
guage."—*Tablet.*

BRIDGETT, REV. T. E. (C.SS.R.)—*continued*.

Ritual of the New Testament. An essay on the prin-
ciples and origin of Catholic Ritual in reference to
the New Testament. Third edition . . . £0 5 0

The Life of the Blessed John Fisher. With a repro-
duction of the famous portrait of Blessed JOHN
FISHER by HOLBEIN, and other Illustrations. 2nd Ed. 0 7 6
"The Life of Blessed John Fisher could hardly fail to be interesting and instructive. Sketched by Father Bridgett's practised pen,
the portrait of this holy martyr is no less vividly displayed in the
printed pages of the book than in the wonderful picture of Holbein,
which forms the frontispiece."—*Tablet.*

The True Story of the Catholic Hierarchy deposed by
Queen Elizabeth, with fuller Memoirs of its Last
Two Survivors. By the Rev. T. E. BRIDGETT,
C.SS.R., and the late Rev. T. F. KNOX, D.D., of
the London Oratory. Crown 8vo, cloth, 0 7 6
" We gladly acknowledge the value of this work on a subject which
has been obscured by prejudice and carelessness."—*Saturday Review.*

The Life and Writings of Sir Thomas More, Lord
Chancellor of England and Martyr under Henry
VIII. With Portrait of the Martyr taken from the
Crayon Sketch made by Holbein in 1527 . . 0 7 6
"Father Bridgett has followed up his valuable Life of Bishop
Fisher with a still more valuable Life of Thomas More. It is, as the
title declares, a study not only of the life, but also of the writings of
Sir Thomas. Father Bridgett has considered him from every point
of view, and the result is, it seems to us, a more complete and
finished portrait of the man, mentally and physically, than has been
hitherto presented."—*Athenæum.*

BRIDGETT, REV. T. E. (C.SS.R.), Edited by.

Souls Departed. By CARDINAL ALLEN. First published in 1565, now edited in modern spelling by the
Rev. T. E. Bridgett 0 6 0

BROWNE, REV. R. D.:

Plain Sermons. Sixty-eight Plain Sermons on the
Fundamental Truths of the Catholic Church.
Crown 8vo 0 6 0
" These are good sermons. . . . The great merit of which is that
they might be read *verbatim* to any congregation, and they would
be understood and appreciated by the uneducated almost as fully as
by the cultured. They have been carefully put together; their
language is simple and their matter is solid."—*Catholic News.*

BUCKLER, REV. H. REGINALD (O.P.)

The Perfection of Man by Charity: a Spiritual
Treatise. Crown 8vo, cloth. . . . 0 5 0
"We have read this unpretending, but solid and edifying work,
with much pleasure, and heartily commend it to our readers. . . .
Its scope is sufficiently explained by the title."—*The Month.*

CASWALL, FATHER.

Catholic Latin Instructor in the Principal Church Offices and Devotions, for the Use of Choirs, Convents, and Mission Schools, and for Self-Teaching. 1 vol., complete £0 3 6

Or Part I., containing Benediction, Mass, Serving at Mass, and various Latin Prayers in ordinary use . 0 1 6

May Pageant : A Tale of Tintern. (A Poem) Second edition 0 2 0

Poems 0 5 0

Lyra Catholica, containing all the Breviary and Missal Hymns, with others from various sources. 32mo, cloth, red edges 0 2 6

CATHOLIC BELIEF: OR, A SHORT AND

Simple Exposition of Catholic Doctrine. By the Very Rev. Joseph Faà di Bruno, D.D. Tenth edition . . . . . Price 6d.; post free, 0 0 8½

Cloth, lettered, ... 0 0 10

Also an edition on better paper and bound in cloth, with gilt lettering and steel frontispiece 0 2 0

CHALLONER, BISHOP.

Meditations for every day in the year. New edition. Revised and edited by the Right Rev. John Virtue, D.D., Bishop of Portsmouth. 8vo. 5th edition . 0 3 0

And in other bindings.

COLERIDGE, REV. H. J. (S.J.) (See Quarterly Series.)

DEVAS, C. S.

Studies of Family Life : a contribution to Social Science. Crown 8vo 0 5 0

"We recommend these pages and the remarkable evidence brought together in them to the careful attention of all who are interested in the well-being of our common humanity."—*Guardian.*

"Both thoughtful and stimulating."—*Saturday Review.*

DRANE, AUGUSTA THEODOSIA.

History of St. Catherine of Siena and her Companions. A new edition in two vols. 0 12 6

"It has been reserved for the author of the present work to give us a complete biography of St. Catherine. . . . Perhaps the greatest success of the writer is the way in which she has contrived to make the Saint herself live in the pages of the book."—*Tablet.*

EYRE, MOST REV. CHARLES, (Abp. of Glasgow).

The History of St. Cuthbert : or, An Account of his Life, Decease, and Miracles. Third edition. Illustrated with maps, charts, &c., and handsomely bound in cloth. Royal 8vo 0 14 0

"A handsome, well appointed volume, in every way worthy of its illustrious subject. . . . The chief impression of the whole is the picture of a great and good man drawn by a sympathetic hand."—*Spectator.*

FABER, REV. FREDERICK WILLIAM, (D.D.)

All for Jesus	£0	5	0
Bethlehem	0	7	0
Blessed Sacrament	0	7	6
Creator and Creature	0	6	0
Ethel's Book of the Angels	0	5	0
Foot of the Cross	0	6	0
Growth in Holiness	0	6	0
Hymns	0	6	0
Notes on Doctrinal and Spiritual Subjects, 2 vols. each	0	5	0
Poems (a new edition in preparation)			
Precious Blood	0	5	0
Sir Lancelot	0	5	0
Spiritual Conferences	0	6	0
Life and Letters of Frederick William Faber, D.D., Priest of the Oratory of St. Philip Neri. By John Edward Bowden of the same Congregation	0	6	0

FOLEY, REV. HENRY, (S.J.)

Records of the English Province of the Society of Jesus. Vol. I., Series I.	net	1	6	0
Vol. II., Series II., III., IV.	net	1	6	0
Vol. III., Series V., VI., VII., VIII.	net	1	10	0
Vol. IV. Series IX., X., XI.	net	1	6	0
Vol. V., Series XII. with nine Photographs of Martyrs	net	1	10	0
Vol. VI., Diary and Pilgrim-Book of the English College, Rome. The Diary from 1579 to 1773, with Biographical and Historical Notes. The Pilgrim-Book of the Ancient English Hospice attached to the College from 1580 to 1656, with Historical Notes	net	1	6	0
Vol. VII. Part the First : General Statistics of the Province ; and Collectanea, giving Biographical Notices of its Members and of many Irish and Scotch Jesuits. With 20 Photographs	net	1	6	0
Vol. VII. Part the Second : Collectanea, Completed ; With Appendices. Catalogues of Assumed and Real Names: Annual Letters ; Biographies and Miscellanea.	net	1	6	0

"As a biographical dictionary of English Jesuits, it deserves a place in every well-selected library, and, as a collection of marvellous occurrences, persecutions, martyrdoms, and evidences of the results of faith, amongst the books of all who belong to the Catholic Church."—*Genealogist.*

FORMBY, REV. HENRY.

Monotheism : in the main derived from the Hebrew nation and the Law of Moses. The Primitive Religion of the City of Rome. An historical Investigation. Demy 8vo.	0	5	0

FRANCIS DE SALES, ST.: THE WORKS OF.
Translated into the English Language by the Very Rev.
Canon Mackey, O.S.B., under the direction of the
Right Rev. Bishop Hedley, O.S.B.   .   .   .
Vol. I. Letters to Persons in the World. Cloth   . £0   6   0
"The letters must be read in order to comprehend the charm and
sweetness of their style."—*Tablet.*
Vol. II.—The Treatise on the Love of God. Father
Carr's translation of 1630 has been taken as a basis,
but it has been modernized and thoroughly revised
and corrected.   0   9   0
"To those who are seeking perfection by the path of contemplation
this volume will be an armoury of help."—*Saturday Review.*
Vol. III. The Catholic Controversy.   .   .   .   0   6   0
"No one who has not read it can conceive how clear, how convinc-
ing, and how well adapted to our present needs are these controversial
'leaves.'"—*Tablet.*
Vol. IV. Letters to Persons in Religion, with introduction by Bishop Hedley on "St. Francis de Sales
and the Religious State."   0   6   0
"The sincere piety and goodness, the grave wisdom, the knowledge
of human nature, the tenderness for its weakness, and the desire for
its perfection that pervade the letters, make them pregnant of instruction for all serious persons. The translation and editing have
been admirably done."—*Scotsman.*
  ⁎ Other vols. in preparation.

GALLWEY, REV. PETER, (S.J.)
Precious Pearl of Hope in the Mercy of God, The.
Translated from the Italian. With Preface by the
Rev. Father Gallwey. Cloth.   0   4   6
Lectures on Ritualism and on the Anglican Orders.
2 vols.   (Or may be had separately.)   0   8   0
Salvage from the Wreck. A few Memories of the
Dead, preserved in Funeral Discourses. With
Portraits. Crown 8vo.   0   7   6

GIBSON, REV. H.
Catechism Made Easy. Being an Explanation of the
Christian Doctrine. Fifth edition. 2 vols., cloth   0   7   6
"This work must be of priceless worth to any who are engaged in
any form of catechetical instruction. It is the best book of the kind
that we have seen in English."—*Irish Monthly.*

GILLOW, JOSEPH.
Literary and Biographical History, or, Bibliographical
Dictionary of the English Catholics. From the
Breach with Rome, in 1534, to the Present Time.
Vols. I., II. and III. cloth, demy 8vo .   . each.   0 15   0
  ⁎ Other vols. in preparation.
"The patient research of Mr. Gillow, his conscientious record of
minute particulars, and especially his exhaustive bibliographical in-
formation in connection with each name, are beyond praise."—*British
Quarterly Review.*
The Haydock Papers. Illustrated. Demy 8vo.   .   0   7   6
" We commend this collection to the attention of every one that
is interested in the records of the sufferings and struggles of our
ancestors to hand down the faith to their children. It is in the
perusal of such details that we bring home to ourselves the truly
heroic sacrifices that our forefathers endured in those dark and
dismal times."—*Tablet.*

GROWTH IN THE KNOWLEDGE OF OUR LORD.

Meditations for every Day in the Year, exclusive of those for Festivals, Days of Retreat, &c. Adapted from the original of Abbé de Brandt, by Sister Mary Fidelis. A new and Improved Edition, in 3 Vols. Sold only in sets. Price per set, ... £1　2　6

"The praise, though high, bestowed on these excellent meditations by the Bishop of Salford is well deserved. The language, like good spectacles, spreads treasures before our vision without attracting attention to itself."—*Dublin Review.*

HEDLEY, BISHOP.

Our Divine Saviour, and other Discourses. Crown 8vo. . . . . o　6　o

"A distinct and noteworthy feature of these sermons is, we certainly think, their freshness—freshness of thought, treatment, and style; nowhere do we meet pulpit commonplace or hackneyed phrase—everywhere, on the contrary, it is the heart of the preacher pouring out to his flock his own deep convictions, enforcing them from the 'Treasures, old and new,' of a cultivated mind."—*Dublin Review.*

HUMPHREY, REV. W. (S.J.)

Suarez on the Religious State : A Digest of the Doctrine contained in his Treatise, "De Statû Religionis." 3 vols., pp. 1200. Cloth, roy. 8vo. . . . 1　10　0

"This laborious and skilfully executed work is a distinct addition to English theological literature. Father Humphrey's style is quiet, methodical, precise, and as clear as the subject admits. Every one will be struck with the air of legal exposition which pervades the book. He takes a grip of his author, under which the text yields up every atom of its meaning and force."—*Dublin Review.*

The One Mediator; or, Sacrifice and Sacraments. Crown 8vo, cloth . . . . o　5　o

"An exceedingly accurate theological exposition of doctrines which are the life of Christianity and which make up the soul of the Christian religion. . . . A profound work, but so far from being dark, obscure, and metaphysical difficulty, the meaning of each paragraph shines with a crystalline clearness."—*Tablet.*

KING, FRANCIS.

The Church of my Baptism, and why I returned to it. Crown 8vo, cloth . . . . . . o　2　6

"A book of the higher controversial criticism. Its literary style is good, its controversial manner excellent, and its writer's emphasis does not escape in italics and notes of exclamation, but is all reserved for lucid and cogent reasoning. Altogether a book of an excellent spirit, written with freshness and distinction."—*Weekly Register.*

LEDOUX, REV. S. M.

History of the Seven Holy Founders of the Order of the Servants of Mary. Crown 8vo, cloth . . o　4　6

"Throws a full light upon the Seven Saints recently canonized, whom we see as they really were. All that was marvellous in their call, their works, and their death is given with the charm of a picturesque and speaking style."—*Messenger of the Sacred Heart.*

LEE, REV. F. G., D.D. (of All Saints, Lambeth.)

Edward the Sixth : Supreme Head. Second edition. Crown 8vo . . . . , . . o　6　o

"In vivid interest and in literary power, no less than in solid historical value, Dr. Lee's present work comes fully up to the standard of its predecessors; and to say that is to bestow high praise. The book evinces Dr. Lee's customary diligence of research in amassing facts, and his rare artistic power in welding them into a harmonious and effective whole."—*John Bull.*

LIGUORI, ST. ALPHONSUS.

New and Improved Translation of the Complete Works
of St. Alphonsus, edited by the late Bishop Coffin :—
Vol. I. The Christian Virtues, and the Means for Obtaining them. Cloth elegant £0   4   0
Or separately :—
   1. The Love of our Lord Jesus Christ   .   .   .   0   1   4
   2. Treatise on Prayer. *(In the ordinary editions a
   great part of this work is omitted)*   .   .   .   0   1   4
   3. A Christian's rule of Life   0   1   0
Vol. II. The Mysteries of the Faith—The Incarnation ;
containing Meditations and Devotions on the Birth
and Infancy of Jesus Christ, &c., suited for Advent
and Christmas.   0   3   6
   Cheap edition   0   2   0
Vol. III. The Mysteries of the Faith—The Blessed
Sacrament   0   3   6
   Cheap edition   0   2   0
Vol. IV. Eternal Truths—Preparation for Death   .   0   3   6
   Cheap edition   0   2   0
Vol. V. The Redemption Meditations on the Passion.   0   3   0
   Cheap edition   0   2   0
   Jesus hath loved us .   .   .   (separately).   0   0   9
Vol. VI. Glories of Mary. New edition .   .   .   0   3   6
   With Frontispiece, cloth   0   4   6

LIVIUS, REV. T. (M.A., C.SS.R.)

St. Peter, Bishop of Rome ; or, the Roman Episcopate
of the Prince of the Apostles, proved from the
Fathers, History and Chronology, and illustrated by
arguments from other sources. Dedicated to his
Eminence Cardinal Newman. Demy 8vo, cloth .   0 12   0
"A book which deserves careful attention. In respect of literary
qualities, such as effective arrangement, and correct and lucid
diction, this essay, by an English Catholic scholar, is not unworthy
of Cardinal Newman, to whom it is dedicated."—*The Sun.*
Explanation of the Psalms and Canticles in the Divine
Office. By ST. ALPHONSUS LIGUORI. Translated
from the Italian by THOMAS LIVIUS, C.SS.R.
With a Preface by his Eminence Cardinal MANNING.
Crown 8vo, cloth   0   7   6
"To nuns and others who know little or no Latin, the book will
be of immense importance."—*Dublin Review.*
"Father Livius has in our opinion even improved on the original,
so far as the arrangement of the book goes. New priests will find
it especially useful."—*Month.*
Mary in the Epistles ; or, The Implicit Teaching of
the Apostles concerning the Blessed Virgin, set
forth in devout comments on their writings.
Illustrated from Fathers and other Authors, and
prefaced by introductory Chapters. Crown 8vo.
Cloth   0   5   0

MANNING, CARDINAL.

England and Christendom	£0	10	6
Four Great Evils of the Day. 5th edition. Wrapper	0	2	6
Cloth	0	3	6
Fourfold Sovereignty of God. 3rd edition. Wrapper	0	2	6
Cloth	0	3	6
Glories of the Sacred Heart. 5th edition . .	0	6	0
Grounds of Faith. Cloth. 9th edition. Wrapper	0	1	0
Cloth	0	1	6
Independence of the Holy See. 2nd edition . .	0	5	0
Internal Mission of the Holy Ghost. 5th edition .	0	8	6
Miscellanies. 3 vols. . . . . the set	0	18	0
National Education. Wrapper	0	2	0
Cloth	0	2	6
Petri Privilegium	0	10	6
Religio Viatoris. 3rd edition, cloth . . .	0	2	0
Wrapper	0	1	0
Sermons on Ecclesiastical Subjects. Vols. I., II., and III. . . . . each	0	6	0
Sin and its Consequences. 7th edition . . .	0	6	0
Temporal Mission of the Holy Ghost. 3rd edition	0	8	6
Temporal Power of the Pope. 3rd edition . .	0	5	0
True Story of the Vatican Council. 2nd edition .	0	5	0
The Eternal Priesthood. 9th edition . . .	0	2	6
The Office of the Church in the Higher Catholic Education. A Pastoral Letter . . .	0	0	6
Workings of the Holy Spirit in the Church of England. Reprint of a letter addressed to Dr. Pusey in 1864 Wrapper	0	1	0
Cloth	0	1	6
Lost Sheep Found. A Sermon	0	0	6
On Education	0	0	3
Rights and Dignity of Labour	0	0	1

The Westminster Series

In handy pocket size.

The Blessed Sacrament, the Centre of Immutable Truth, Wrapper	0	0	6
Confidence in God. Wrapper	0	1	0
Or the two bound together. Cloth . .	0	2	0
Holy Gospel of Our Lord Jesus Christ according to St. John. Cloth	0	1	0
Holy Ghost the Sanctifier. Cloth . . .	0	2	0
Love of Jesus to Penitents. Wrapper . .	0	1	0
Cloth	0	1	6
Office of the Holy Ghost under the Gospel. Cloth	0	1	0

MANNING, CARDINAL, Edited by.

Life of the Curé of Ars. Popular edition . . .	0	2	6

MEDAILLE, REV. P.

Meditations on the Gospels for Every Day in the
Year. Translated into English from the new Edition, enlarged by the Besançon Missionaries, under
the direction of the Rev. W. H. Eyre, S.J. Cloth £0 6 0
(This work has already been translated into Latin,
Italian, Spanish, German, and Dutch.)
"We have carefully examined these Meditations, and are fain to
confess that we admire them very much. They are short, succinct,
pithy, always to the point, and wonderfully suggestive."—*Tablet.*

MIVART, PROF. ST. GEORGE (M.D., F.R.S.)

Nature and Thought. Second edition .   .   .   0 4 0
"The complete command of the subject, the wide grasp, the
subtlety, the readiness of illustration, the grace of style, contrive
to render this one of the most admirable books of its class."—
British Quarterly Review.

A Philosophical Catechism. Fifth edition .   0 1 0
"It should become the *vade mecum* of Catholic students."—*Tablet.*

MONTGOMERY, HON. MRS.

*Approved by the Most Rev. George Porter, Archbishop of
Bombay.*

The Divine Sequence : A Treatise on Creation and
Redemption. Cloth 0 3 6
The Eternal Years. With an Introduction by the
Most Rev. George Porter, Archbishop of Bombay.
Cloth 0 3 6
The Divine Ideal. Cloth 0 3 6
"A work of original thought carefully developed and expressed in
lucid and richly imaged style."—*Tablet.*
"The writing of a pious, thoughtful, earnest woman."—*Church
Review.*
"Full of truth, and sound reason, and confidence."—*American
Catholic Book News.*

MORRIS, REV. JOHN (S.J.)

Letter Books of Sir Amias Poulet, keeper of Mary
Queen of Scots. Demy 8vo 0 10 6
Troubles of our Catholic Forefathers, related by themselves. Second Series. 8vo, cloth.   .   .   .   0 14 0
    Third Series 0 14 0
The Life of Father John Gerard, S.J. Third edition,
rewritten and enlarged 0 14 0
The Life and Martyrdom of St. Thomas Becket. Second
and enlarged edition. In one volume, large post 8vo,
cloth, pp. xxxvi., 632, ...   0 12 6
or bound in two parts, cloth 0 13 0

MORRIS, REV. W. B. (of the Oratory.)

The Life of St. Patrick, Apostle of Ireland. Fourth
edition. Crown 8vo, cloth 0 5 0
"The secret of Father Morris's success is, that he has got the
proper key to the extraordinary, the mysterious life and character of
St. Patrick. He has taken the Saint's own authentic writings as
the foundation whereon to build."—*Irish Ecclesiastical Record.*
"Promises to become the standard biography of Ireland's Apostle.
For clear statement of facts, and calm judicious discussion of con-
troverted points, it surpasses any work we know of in the literature
of the subject."—*American Catholic Quarterly.*

NEWMAN, CARDINAL.

Church of the Fathers £0 4 0
Prices of other works by Cardinal Newman on
application.

PAGANI, VERY REV. JOHN BAPTIST,

The Science of the Saints in Practice. By John Baptist Pagani, Second General of the Institute of
Charity. Complete in three volumes. Vol. 1,
January to April. Vol. 2, May to August. Vol. 3,
September to December . . . . each   0 5 0
"'The Science of the Saints' is a practical treatise on the principal
Christian virtues, abundantly illustrated with interesting examples
from Holy Scripture as well as from the Lives of the Saints. Written
chiefly for devout souls, such as are trying to live an interior and supernatural life by following in the footsteps of our Lord and His saints,
this work is eminently adapted for the use of ecclesiastics and of religious communities."—*Irish Ecclesiastical Record.*

PAYNE, JOHN ORLEBAR, (M.A.)

Records of the English Catholics of 1715. Demy 8vo.
Half-bound, gilt top 0 15 0
"A book of the kind Mr. Payne has given us would have astonish-
ed Bishop Milner or Dr. Lingard. They would have treasured it,
for both of them knew the value of minute fragments of historical
information. The Editor has derived nearly the whole of the information which he has given, from unprinted sources, and we must
congratulate him on having found a few incidents here and there
which may bring the old times back before us in a most touching
manner."—*Tablet.*

English Catholic Non-Jurors of 1715. Being a Sum-
mary of the Register of their Estates, with Genea-
logical and other Notes, and an Appendix of
Unpublished Documents in the Public Record
Office. In one Volume. Demy 8vo. . .   1 1 0
"Most carefully and creditably brought out . . . From first to last,
full of social interest and biographical details, for which we may
search in vain elsewhere."—*Antiquarian Magazine.*

Old English Catholic Missions. Demy 8vo, half-bound.   0 7 6
"A book to hunt about in for curious odds and ends."—*Saturday
Review.*
"These registers tell us in their too brief records, teeming with inter-
est for all their scantiness, many a tale of patient heroism."—*Tablet.*

POOR SISTERS OF NAZARETH, THE.

A descriptive Sketch of Convent Life. By Alice Meynell.
Profusely Illustrated with Drawings especially made
by George Lambert. Large 4to. Boards . .   0 2 6
A limited number of copies are also issued as an *Edition
de Luxe*, containing proofs of the illustrations printed
on one side only of the paper, and handsomely bound.   0 10 6
"Bound in a most artistic cover, illustrated with a naturalness
that could only have been born of powerful sympathy; printed clearly,
neatly, and on excellent paper, and written with the point, aptness,
and ripeness of style which we have learnt to associate with Mrs.
Meynell's literature."—*Tablet.*

QUARTERLY SERIES   Edited by the Rev. H. J. Coleridge, S.J.   76 volumes published to date.
Selection.

The Life and Letters of St. Francis Xavier. By the Rev. H. J. Coleridge, S.J. 2 vols. . . .	£0	10	6
The History of the Sacred Passion. By Father Luis de la Palma, of the Society of Jesus. Translated from the Spanish.	0	5	0
The Life of Dona Louisa de Carvajal. By Lady Georgiana Fullerton. Small edition . . .	0	3	6
The Life and Letters of St. Teresa. 3 vols. By Rev. H. J. Coleridge, S.J. . . . . each	0	7	6
The Life of Mary Ward. By Mary Catherine Elizabeth Chalmers, of the Institute of the Blessed Virgin. Edited by the Rev. H. J. Coleridge, S.J. 2 vols.	0	15	0
The Return of the King. Discourses on the Latter Days. By the Rev. H. J. Coleridge, S.J. . .	0	7	6
Pious Affections towards God and the Saints. Meditations for every Day in the Year, and for the Principal Festivals. From the Latin of the Ven. Nicolas Lancicius, S.J.	0	7	6
The Life and Teaching of Jesus Christ in Meditations for Every Day in the Year. By Fr. Nicolas Avancino, S.J. Two vols.	0	10	6
The Baptism of the King : Considerations on the Sacred Passion. By the Rev. H. J. Coleridge, S.J. .	0	7	6
The Mother of the King. Mary during the Life of Our Lord.	0	7	6
The Hours of the Passion. Taken from the *Life of Christ* by Ludolph the Saxon	0	7	6
The Mother of the Church. Mary during the first Apostolic Age	0	6	0
The Life of St. Bridget of Sweden. By the late F. J. M. A. Partridge	0	6	0
The Teachings and Counsels of St. Francis Xavier. From his Letters	0	5	0
Garcia Moreno, President of Ecuador. 1821—1875. From the French of the Rev. P. A. Berthe, C.SS.R. By Lady Herbert	0	7	6
The Life of St. Alonso Rodriguez. By Francis Goldie, of the Society of Jesus	0	7	6
Letters of St. Augustine. Selected and arranged by Mary H. Allies	0	6	6
A Martyr from the Quarter-Deck—Alexis Clerc, S.J. By Lady Herbert	0	5	0

VOLUMES ON THE LIFE OF OUR LORD.
The Holy Infancy.

The Preparation of the Incarnation	0	7	6
The Nine Months. The Life of our Lord in the Womb.	0	7	6
The Thirty Years. Our Lord's Infancy and Early Life.	0	7	6

The Public Life of Our Lord.

The Ministry of St. John Baptist . . .	0	6	6

QUARTERLY SERIES—*(selection) continued.*

The Preaching of the Beatitudes	£0	6	6
The Sermon on the Mount. Continued. 2 Parts, each	0	6	6
The Training of the Apostles. Parts I., II., III., IV. each	0	6	6
The Preaching of the Cross. Part I. . .	0	6	6
The Preaching of the Cross. Parts II., III. each	0	6	0
Passiontide. Parts I. II. and III., each . . .	0	6	6
Chapters on the Parables of Our Lord . . .	0	7	6

Introductory Volumes.

The Life of our Life. Harmony of the Life of Our Lord, with Introductory Chapters and Indices. Second edition. Two vols.	0	15	0
The Works and Words of our Saviour, gathered from the Four Gospels	0	7	6
The Story of the Gospels. Harmonised for Meditation	0	7	6

Full lists on application.

RAM, MRS. ABEL.

"Emmanuel." Being the Life of Our Lord Jesus Christ reproduced in the Mysteries of the Tabernacle. By Mrs. Abel Ram, author of "The most Beautiful among the Children of Men," &c. Crown 8vo, cloth   0   5   0

"The foundation of the structure is laid with the greatest skill and the deepest knowledge of what constitutes true religion, and every chapter ends with an eloquent and soul-inspiring appeal for one or other of the virtues which the different scenes in the life of Our Saviour set prominently into view."—*Catholic Times.*

RICHARDS, REV. WALTER J. B. (D.D.)

Manual of Scripture History. Being an Analysis of the Historical Books of the Old Testament. By the Rev. W. J. B. Richards, D.D., Oblate of St. Charles ; Inspector of Schools in the Diocese of Westminster. Cloth   0   4   0

"Happy indeed will those children and young persons be who acquire in their early days the inestimably precious knowledge which these books impart."—*Tablet.*

RYDER, REV. H. I. D. (of the Oratory.)

Catholic Controversy: A Reply to Dr. Littledale's "Plain Reasons." Sixth edition   0   2   6

"Father Ryder of the Birmingham Oratory, has now furnished in a small volume a masterly reply to this assailant from without. The lighter charms of a brilliant and graceful style are added to the solid merits of this handbook of contemporary controversy."—*Irish Monthly.*

SOULIER, REV. P.

Life of St. Philip Benizi, of the Order of the Servants of Mary. Crown 8vo   0   8   0

"A clear and interesting account of the life and labours of this eminent Servant of Mary."—*American Catholic Quarterly.*
"Very scholar-like, devout and complete."—*Dublin Review.*

STANTON, REV. R. (of the Oratory.)
A Menology of England and Wales ; or, Brief Mem-
orials of the British and English Saints, arranged
according to the Calendar. Together with the Martyrs of the 16th and 17th centuries. Compiled by
order of the Cardinal Archbishop and the Bishops
of the Province of Westminster.   Demy 8vo, cloth   £0 14   0

THOMPSON, EDWARD HEALY, (M.A.)
The Life of Jean-Jacques Olier, Founder of the
Seminary of St. Sulpice. New and Enlarged Edition.
Post 8vo, cloth, pp. xxxvi. 628   .   .   .   .   .   0 15   0

*" It provides us with just what we most need, a model to look up to
and imitate ; one whose circumstances and surroundings were sufficiently like our own to admit of an easy and direct application to our
own personal duties and daily occupations."—Dublin Review.*

The Life and Glories of St. Joseph, Husband of
Mary, Foster-Father of Jesus, and Patron of the
Universal Church. Grounded on the Dissertations of
Canon Antonio Vitalis, Father José Moreno, and other
writers.   Crown 8vo, cloth, pp. xxvi., 488,   .   .   0   6   0

ULLATHORNE, ARCHBISHOP.
Endowments of Man, &c.   Popular edition.   .   .   0   7   0
Groundwork of the Christian Virtues : do.   .   .   0   7   0
Christian Patience,   .   .   do. do.   .   .   0   7   0
Ecclesiastical Discourses   0   6   0
Memoir of Bishop Willson.   0   2   6

VAUGHAN, ARCHBISHOP, (O.S.B.)
The Life and Labours of St. Thomas of Aquin.
Abridged and edited by Dom Jerome Vaughan,
O.S.B.   Second Edition.   (Vol. I., Benedictine
Library.)   Crown 8vo.   Attractively bound   .   .   0   6   6

*" Popularly written, in the best sense of the word, skilfully avoids
all wearisome detail, whilst omitting nothing that is of importance
in the incidents of the Saint's existence, or for a clear understanding
of the nature and the purpose of those sublime theological works
on which so many Pontiffs, and notably Leo XIII., have pronounced
such remarkable and repeated commendations."—Freeman's Journal.*

WARD, WILFRID.
The Clothes of Religion. A reply to popular Positivism.   0   3   6
"Very witty and interesting."—Spectator.
*"Really models of what such essays should be."—Church Quarterly
Review.*

WATERWORTH, REV. J.
The Canons and Decrees of the Sacred and Œcumenical
Council of Trent, celebrated under the Sovereign
Pontiffs, Paul III., Julius III., and Pius IV., tran-
slated by the Rev. J. WATERWORTH.   To which
are prefixed Essays on the External and Internal
History of the Council. A new edition. Demy
8vo, cloth 0 10   6

WISEMAN, CARDINAL.
Fabiola.   A Tale of the Catacombs. . .   3s. 6d. and   0   4   0
Also a new and splendid edition printed on large
quarto paper, embellished with thirty-one full-page
illustrations, and a coloured portrait of St. Agnes.
Handsomely bound.   1   1   0

www.ingramcontent.com/pod-product-compliance
Lightning Source LLC
Chambersburg PA
CBHW031955060726
47497CB00016B/2305